"I LIKE YOUR HAIR LOOSE LIKE THIS."

"You kept fiddling with the ends." Rio picked up a strand of her hair from the side of her face and rubbed it between his thumb and fingers. "Like this."

Yasmine smiled self-consciously. "It's an old habit. Usually I'm not even aware that I'm doing it."

"It's a sensual gesture," he said softly, "and it's also a little-girl gesture. A man could go crazy trying to figure it out." He gently tugged on her hand, drawing her out of the lantern light and into the shadows of the spreading oak. Then almost leisurely he pulled her against him, lowered his head, and covered her mouth with his.

She wasn't surprised by his kiss or even by her reaction to it.

His lips on hers were firm, demanding, his tongue against hers seductive and daring. She was aware only of him and the desire he was making her feel.

He lifted his head and raised a shaking hand to stroke her hair. "Come home with me, Yasmine," he said huskily. "Spend the night with me, make love with me."

WHAT ARE *LOVESWEPT* ROMANCES?

They are stories of true romance and touching emotion. We believe those two very important ingredients are constants in our highly sensual and very believable stories in the LOVE-SWEPT line. Our goal is to give you, the reader, stories of consistently high quality that may sometimes make you laugh, sometimes make you cry, but are always fresh and creative and contain many delightful surprises within their pages.

Most romance fans read an enormous number of books. Those they truly love, they keep. Others may be traded with friends and soon forgotten. We hope that each LOVESWEPT romance will be a treasure—a "keeper." We will always try to publish

LOVE STORIES YOU'LL NEVER FORGET
BY AUTHORS YOU'LL ALWAYS REMEMBER

The Editors

Loveswept® 838

The Damaron Mark:

THE
HEIRESS

FAYRENE
PRESTON

BANTAM BOOKS
NEW YORK · TORONTO · LONDON · SYDNEY · AUCKLAND

THE DAMARON MARK: THE HEIRESS
A Bantam Book / June 1997

ISBN 0-553-44533-2

Published simultaneously in the United States and Canada

Bantam Books are published by Bantam Books, a division of Bantam Dou-
bleday Dell Publishing Group, Inc. Its trademark, consisting of the words
"Bantam Books" and the portrayal of a rooster, is Registered in U.S.
Patent and Trademark Office and in other countries. Marca Registrada.
Bantam Books, 1540 Broadway, New York, New York 10036.

PRINTED IN THE UNITED STATES OF AMERICA

OPM   10 9 8 7 6 5 4 3 2 1

AUTHOR'S NOTE

Happy Birthday, Loveswept, and congratulations! You're fourteen years old! That's quite an accomplishment.

And you know what's even more amazing? None of us looks a day older—not the authors, not the editors, and certainly not you, the readers. In fact, I actually think we may even look *younger*.

Don't you agree?

Well, I tried, okay?

But even though we all may be a few years older, we've had a great time, haven't we? I know I have, and along the way I've also had a lot of wonderful adventures through reading all the marvelous Loveswept stories that have been published in the last fourteen years and through writing my own.

Over the years, I've written about many exciting heroes, heroines, and their families, but the

Damaron family is proving to be one of my favorites. They're an exciting, adventurous, and most of all passionate family made up entirely of cousins who have been welded together by tragedy, love, and the Damaron Mark. I hope you'll read all their stories and that you'll grow to love them as much as I have.

To those of you who have been with us since Loveswept's beginning—thank you!

To those of you who are just discovering us—welcome!

Many exciting ideas loom on the horizon. Fabulous stories written by superbly talented authors will be coming. And the best thing is, there's no end in sight.

Thank you, Loveswept, for fourteen wonderful years!

Fayrene Preston

ONE

"Heads up!" A half-eaten apple flew from one side of the big room to the other.

"Oh, man, you are extremely doomed!" A tennis ball zoomed back in retaliation.

"You need major psychopharmaceuticals if you believe that."

Laughter erupted, a crushed soda can took flight, and a rapid-fire fusillade of paper wads suddenly filled the air.

Yasmine Damaron halted just inside the door as rock music and the smell of coffee and popcorn made a run at her senses.

"Awesome!"

The excited shout drew her attention to a nearby alcove, where three video arcade games beeped and flashed. At the end of the room, an old sci-fi movie unrolled on a giant-screen TV. Crumpled fast-food bags overflowed from a trash basket, in-line skates from another. Five well-used surf-boards were propped against a dented, scraped-up file cabinet.

Jeans, T-shirts, and athletic shoes were the apparel of choice for the dozen mostly-young men and women Yasmine could see, all busy working or playing, with the exception of the curvy redhead lying on a nearby couch, sound asleep despite the activity and noise level.

Yasmine felt positively overdressed in her custom-designed taupe pantsuit. And as for hair, the young women showed an inclination toward punk styles; one even sported purple hair paint. Quite a contrast with the simple pale gold ribbon Yasmine had woven through her braided topaz-colored hair and tied into a neat bow at the end, halfway down her back.

Her golden-eyed gaze wandered on. No partitions divided the large space into separate cubicles. Instead, four rows of desks were centered in the room, their tops hidden beneath an array of computers, modems, printers, and various other electronic equipment, along with comic books, plastic liter bottles of caffeine-laden sodas, and stacks of compact discs.

A slight smile touched her lips. A person would be forgiven for thinking she had wandered into a college dorm rec room, but Yasmine knew better. This room, located in a nondescript building in the Texas hill country outside Austin, was part of Thornton Software, the current epicenter of the multimedia software industry, and the people who worked there were known as Thornton's Young Guns.

"That's it, man. Prepare to die!"

"What fairy tale are you living in?"

"Ramborama!"

"Okay, stand back. I'm about to get explosive!"

"In whose lifetime?"

Heavens, but they made her feel old, Yasmine reflected, though she was only twenty-nine. They also made her feel almost invisible, because, with few exceptions, they were all so engrossed in what they were doing, they hadn't even noticed her.

Her gaze paused on a sign that cautioned DO NOT PLAY WITH THE THERMONUCLEAR WEAPONS, then continued till she saw a big plywood tombstone displayed prominently on a bookshelf. Etched into it were the words DAMARON INTERNATIONAL. She stared at it for several moments.

Then across the room a point of stillness caught her attention. Wide double doors stood open to reveal an office interior. Inside, a man sat with his boots propped on his desk, a keyboard on his lap, and his back to everyone. He seemed lost in his own world as he stared in intense concentration at his monitor. He was calmness amid the commotion, and interestingly, oddly, he was also the center of the room's energy.

Rio Thornton, she instantly concluded—the eccentric nonconformist and, according to some, brilliant man responsible for several of the computer software industry quakes in the last couple of years. And the man she was there to see.

She successfully made it across the big room without drawing fire or any undue attention. Now, if only the next part of her appointment would go as smoothly, she thought wryly, gazing with interest at Rio Thornton's broad back and noting the haphazard, irregular layers of his ash-brown hair that reached midway down his neck. He obviously had no time for stylists or even a regular barber. The information she'd gleaned from her research on him had been correct.

"Excuse me," she said, then realized his concentration was so complete, he hadn't heard her. She lightly touched his shoulder. "Rio Thornton?"

His gray eyes were preoccupied as he slowly turned his head and looked up at her, but at the sight of her, they focused, sharpened, and with a few swift strokes on the keyboard, he wiped his computer screen clear. "How did you get in here?" he asked curtly. With a frown he shifted the keyboard to the desk and craned his neck to glance past her.

She understood the precaution and didn't take offense. "Your assistant buzzed me through. She said you were expecting me."

"She was wrong. Who are you?"

His voice was cool and quiet, but she had no problem hearing him above the din coming from the next room. "I'm Yasmine Damaron."

"Damaron?" His gaze swept over her, touched

on the streak of silver that sliced through her long, topaz-colored hair, then returned to her face. "So it appears."

"So it *is*," she said dryly, her lips quirked with amusement. Her research had prepared her for a less-than-enthusiastic reception, and the fake tombstone in the other room had bolstered that certainty.

"I have an appointment with you," she said. "Didn't you know?"

"Probably." Without taking his gaze from her, he swung his boots off the desk and unfolded his lanky six-foot-one-inch length from the chair to stand so that she now had to look up at him. Her heart gave a hard thud that jarred her entire body.

She believed in being prepared, and to that end she'd read every article on him she could find. She'd even talked to a few people who had met him. But nothing she'd read or been told had come close to capturing the man standing before her.

She was accustomed to the palpable masculinity of the men in her family, but there was nothing obvious or conspicuous about Rio Thornton—not his strength, not his intelligence, and certainly not his sexual appeal, yet it was all there. It was careless, offhand, and subtle, and all the more powerful because it was not forced or planned for effect.

She didn't like surprises, but now she had to face a big one. Her assessment of Rio Thornton was not at all cerebral but, rather, visceral. Her senses were in control, not her brain, and to her chagrin she realized he was having an impact on her as a man instead of as someone with whom she was about to do business.

Try as she might, she couldn't help noticing that the jeans he wore clung to the long, lean lines of his hips and legs in the intimate way of a garment washed and worn many times. His blue T-shirt, so faded she could make out only a couple of the letters of the words that had once been written there, molded his chest in the same revealing way. At least a day's growth of beard shadowed his jaw.

And just when she thought she'd taken in everything about him she could and was on her way to dealing with his effect on her, she caught a glimpse of a weariness and a wariness in his eyes.

He was a relatively young man—thirty-four according to the articles she'd read. He was in command of his own destiny with a brilliant future ahead of him. Maybe he'd been working around the clock, as she'd read he sometimes did, but it made no sense to her that he would be wary of her.

She mentally pulled herself together. "I'm sorry if you weren't expecting me, but I made the appointment a week ago through Penny, your assistant, and since I'm here now—"

Abruptly he twisted to yank a sticky note off his computer. He quickly scanned it, then wadded it up and tossed it into the wastebasket and yanked off another note. Reading it, he nodded. "This is from Penny to remind me that you're coming at two."

"It's two."

"Then you're right on time." The note followed the other into the wastebasket.

Unaccountably entertained, she smiled. "I usually am."

His gaze slid over her body, then returned to her face, and for the first time Yasmine saw humor lighten his eyes. Gray with green flecks, she now noticed.

"I okayed your appointment over a week ago when the request came through, Ms. Damaron, but at the time I was under the impression a Damaron International executive would be coming, rather than an actual Damaron."

"An actual Damaron?" It sounded so funny, she couldn't help but chuckle. "You mean as opposed to a fake one?"

A smile never touched his lips. "I mean as opposed to a representative of Damaron International."

She couldn't make up her mind if he had a sense of humor and just wasn't using it with her, or if he didn't have one at all. Either way, she decided it best to rein in her amusement. Her business with him was important. "I'm very sorry if there was a mix-up over who was coming."

He shrugged. "Things like that happen, and no matter what, I would have still forgotten it. It's been busy around here."

"I see." Her last name not only opened doors around the world, it assured no one ever forgot the time and date of her arrival. *Up until now*. Rio Thornton was definitely a new experience for her as well as an extremely disconcerting one. At least she had the answer to his weariness. "So you've been working so hard that you forgot to read your reminder notes?"

Slowly, gradually, a smile spread across his face, a smile completely without guile that just about knocked the breath out of her. It was the first hint that he possessed an offbeat, effortless charm, though she did remember one report mentioning a certain charisma about him. Another case of the image that had been painted for her by words failing to live up to the reality.

"Don't take it personally," he drawled. "I find my day goes a lot smoother if I don't read my messages."

"I can see where it would." The idea of coming back after she'd done more research on him tempted her, except she was positive she'd depleted all her sources. And she was equally positive that if she left, she wouldn't get another appointment. She was beginning to understand why the average businessperson might have a hard time dealing with him. There was nothing conventional about Rio Thornton.

Without taking his gaze from her, he snagged a tennis ball out of the air before it could connect with the side of his head.

She shook hers in amazement at the chaos that

continued behind her. "Have you ever thought of getting an air traffic controller in here?"

Again he smiled at her. "Would you believe we've never had a single unplanned midair collision?"

"Unplanned?" She chuckled. "Yes, I would believe that." Absently she pulled her braid over her shoulder, reached for one end of the gold ribbon, and fingered it. It was an almost unconscious habit, dating back to when she was a child, but she saw his eyes narrow in on the gesture and she released the ribbon. She waved her hand toward the big room. "I've heard stories about the unique creative environment you've set up here."

"We all work hard, sometimes around the clock. Sometimes we're here for days. Every once in a while we need to play."

"And sleep?" She turned to point to the young woman who was still sound asleep.

Without looking away from her, he nodded. Now that she had his attention, she reflected wryly, she *really* had his attention. But interestingly and maybe a bit irritatingly, he was studying her as if she were a piece of equipment he was taking apart rather than a woman he was finding attractive.

He absently tossed the tennis ball into the air and caught it. "So, Ms. Damaron—what is it that I can do for you?"

His question jolted her. She'd been concentrating so hard on Rio the man, she'd come close to forgetting Rio the owner of Thornton Software, along with the reason she was there. It wasn't like her at all. "To start with, you can call me Yasmine."

He nodded. "Done, Yasmine—and please call me Rio. What else?"

He was being all business with her, which was good, she told herself. "You can give me a few minutes of your time."

He gestured with the tennis ball to a chair on the same side of the desk as his. "Make yourself comfortable."

She glanced over her shoulder at the big room. "Could we please shut the doors?"

Something flashed in his eyes. Wariness again? She suddenly realized that despite his casual demeanor, he was on guard against her and she wondered why. He had nothing to fear from her. Did he? One more thing that didn't make sense to her. Without comment he closed the doors, muting the level of voices and music.

She took the seat he'd indicated, then gave herself a moment to register the stacks of notebooks, manuals, and boxes of software stacked around the perimeter of the office. The only items she saw that might be personal were two photographs on the wall behind the desk.

When she returned her attention to him, she found him leaning back in his chair, relaxed. His gaze was fixed firmly on her. He didn't appear to like pleasantries and small talk, but perversely, she wasn't yet ready to get to the point of her visit.

"I've been looking forward to meeting you for some time, Rio."

"I'm flattered."

"That would be nice if it were true, but somehow, I don't think it is."

"Maybe so," he said in his quiet, slow drawl. "Then again, it's not every day a Damaron comes calling."

A Damaron. He wasn't viewing her as a woman, or even as an individual, but, rather, as merely a part of her family's company. It rankled. "Maybe not a Damaron," she said, "but I know of at least three high-ranking officers of Fortune 500 companies that have. The word is they got nowhere with you."

"I didn't like where they wanted to go."

She nodded, having heard the outcome of the meetings from an inside source, but she was interested in his viewpoint. "And where was that?"

"They wanted me to climb into bed with them." He paused, then said softly, "Is that why you're here, Yasmine? Did you come all the way down here to Texas to ask me to climb into bed with you?"

Her heart gave a hard thud, and the words hung in the air between them. He had used a simple business metaphor, she told herself firmly, but it had nevertheless startled her. Mentally she scrambled to regroup.

She reached for an end of the gold satin ribbon and fingered it. "The timing for this appointment was convenient for me. I was already scheduled to visit friends in the area, and I thought I'd kill two birds with one stone."

His brows shot up. "You kill birds, Yasmine?"

She now understood perfectly why the reports she'd read had described him as "difficult at times." It would have been virtually impossible to be prepared for this man, she decided, and continued as if he hadn't spoken. "My friends have just moved into a new home they built about twenty miles from here."

"How nice for them."

"Rachel and Brent McLain," she said, doggedly supplying unasked-for information. "They've told me that they belong to the same health club as you."

He gave a slight incline of his head.

So much for her attempt at small talk with him, she thought. She'd had the idea that gaining control of the conversation would give her a slight advantage, but in the end it wouldn't matter who had control. She'd still get what she wanted from him. "Okay, Rio, I'll get right to the point. I'm here because Damaron International is extremely interested in your company."

The slow smile he gave sent an equally slow trail of heat down her spine.

"So—the little mosquito must have finally irritated the big giant once too often, huh?"

"Irritated? No. Made us curious and interested

in you? Yes. You cannot steal three contracts out from under our noses and expect us to ignore you."

"I've never had any expectations of Damaron International one way or another," he said, shifting to prop one leg on the opposite knee. "And I didn't *steal* those contracts from you. I *won* them fairly and squarely."

"Actually, Rio," she said, her tone dry, "your bids have come in so low and undercut us so badly, they made us *feel* as if you were stealing from us."

"You may find this hard to believe, but my world doesn't revolve around Damaron International. I'm going after the *contracts*, not your company."

"Which is essentially the same thing. And I don't believe Damaron International is as unimportant to you as you say."

"And why's that?"

"Because in the adjoining room, you have a tombstone with Damaron International engraved on it."

For a moment he looked blank. Then suddenly he threw back his head and laughed, genuinely, heartily. Listening, she felt as if she'd received a treat, a glimpse behind the guard and into the real Rio Thornton. She wanted to hear more of the sound, but too quickly his laughter died away.

He shook his head. "I'd forgotten about that. The first time we managed to undercut your company on a bid, one of the guys got a little carried away and put that up."

"I see. And what did you do to celebrate the second time?"

"We took the weekend off and went surfing."

She nodded. "I saw the boards in the other room."

"We like to keep them close. We never know when the mood will strike."

"Or when you'll walk out the front door and see waves?"

He grinned at her with something like approval, and she thought she might have truly made a connection with him. It was a good feeling, and, she mentally hastened to add, a good portent for their business dealings.

"We live in hope," he said in agreement, his gaze thoughtful. "And you never know—the world is full of surprises."

"Yes, it is," she murmured. Too many for her liking. "So what did you do when you won this last contract, the Borggeo-Wagner contract?"

Abruptly the connection broke and the puzzling guard returned. "We're delaying our celebration until we've completed the contract." He shifted, every line of his body radiating impatience. "Okay, Yasmine, let's get down to it. Winning and losing contracts is part of running a business, so why are you here? To tell me to stop walking away with your contracts?"

"Would it do any good?" she asked half seriously.

"You could always try."

Oddly enough, she wanted to do just that—to tell him to *stop* viewing her as if she were the enemy and not a woman, to *stop* whatever it was he was doing that made her heart beat faster and her mouth go dry just by looking at him. But that particular problem was entirely hers, not his. Later, she promised herself, she'd figure it all out, but for now she had important business to conduct. "As I've already said, I'm here because we're very interested in you and your company."

He gestured at her with the tennis ball. "I'll save you a lot of time and trouble, Yasmine. There's no secret to how I can undercut Damaron International. I run a bone-lean operation."

"You're right—that's no secret. But your operation is not the only reason or even the main reason you continue to get the contracts. It's *you*." She drew in a quiet breath. "Which is why, Rio, we want to buy your company, with the proviso that you stay on with the company and run it."

She could see no surprise on his face. He simply gazed at her for a time, while the silence between them lengthened. She didn't look away from him, but nerves danced along her skin at his laserlike focus on her.

Finally he spoke. "Well, well, well, Yasmine—it turns out you *do* want me to climb into your bed after all."

Unbidden, unwanted, sensual images played through her mind. She saw him drawing her down onto a bed with him, taking her clothes off piece by piece, and making hard, slow love to her until their naked skin glistened with sweat. The images were exciting, frightening, inappropriate, and completely uncharacteristic of her.

Deliberately and with great care, she pulled a folded piece of paper from her purse and pushed it across the desk to him. "This is our offer—the total cash amount. Your signature would be a preliminary agreement to this amount, then your lawyers and ours would meet and hammer out the rest of the details."

He didn't even glance at the paper. "I hope the friends you came to see are good ones."

He'd spoken so quietly, it took her a moment to realize what he'd said. "Why?"

"Because otherwise your trip will be a complete waste. My company is not for sale, and neither am I."

"You haven't even looked at our offer, Rio."

"I don't need to." He pitched the tennis ball into a corner basket that also held a basketball. The tennis ball bounced out and continued bouncing, each movement smaller than the last until finally it rolled away under the desk. He folded his hands together across his stomach. "Damaron International must be in a bad way if it can't stand even a small amount of competition."

"Damaron International could lose contracts for the next fifty years and still not be in a bad way."

A slight smile touched his lips. "Exactly. So why do you want me—and my company?"

His suddenly suggestive tone made her feel the need to separate herself from the company. "It's Damaron International that wants you and your company."

"Oh? Sorry, my mistake. I thought you were here representing your family's company."

He was being deliberately difficult. "Listen to me, Rio. I don't need to tell you that the landscape of the computer business is constantly changing— it's an ongoing revolution, pure and simple. To stay on its cutting edge, you have to be creative and nimble, and you've proven yourself to be one of the best at that, if not *the* best. That's why DI wants you."

His smile faded. "If I was interested in selling, Yasmine, I would have sold to one of those other companies."

"Their offers can't even be considered in the same ballpark as ours. Look at ours"—she pointed to the paper—"and you'll see just how much we want you." She knew immediately she'd used the wrong phrasing, and she rushed to add, "How much we value you."

His gaze lowered to her lips and lingered. "It's very nice to be wanted by you, Yasmine, and I'm sure there are a lot of men who'd love to hear those words from your lips, but I'm not one of them."

He was speaking of business, yet for some reason he was intentionally infusing an intimacy into the conversation. She supposed it could be called sexual harassment, something she'd never had to deal with before because of who she was. But she didn't believe that Rio was truly coming on to her.

Basically he was simply being a first-class jerk, trying to throw her off stride, put her at a disadvantage, and run her off. The question was *why*.

Normally when she didn't have control of a situation, she would begin to panic, but in this case Rio had just flat out made her angry and more than ever determined to win. "I would appreciate it if you would take the offer seriously. This is a legitimate business offer, Rio."

"And I am *legitimately* not interested, Yasmine."

She hadn't expected to win this first round, but she hadn't anticipated the sheer frustration she felt at losing it either. "Don't you even want to look at the offer?"

"Not really."

She was amazed. She'd never encountered anyone or anything like Rio Thornton.

"But I do have a question."

Okay, she thought—questions showed interest. Perhaps it was a good sign. "What's that?"

"How much do you have to do with the offer?"

Her brow furrowed. "I'm not sure I understand what you're asking."

He nodded toward the piece of paper that lay between them. "Are those your figures?"

Her face cleared. "Ah, I see—you want to know how much power I have to back up my offer."

"No, that's not it. I'm sure you have a great deal of power. I want to know how *personal* this is for you. In other words, how much of *yourself* do you have invested in this offer?"

It was a very strange question and she wasn't sure how to answer it. "Well, I was the one who researched your company and who came up with the very substantial figure on that piece of paper that you haven't even bothered to look at."

"And how did you do that?"

"Do what?"

"How did you decide what dollar amount to put on me?"

"I—" She shook her head, knowing he was trying to confuse her. "It's not an offer for you as a man."

"Yasmine, Yasmine"—he shook his head—"you've already admitted that it's *me* you want, so therefore you're making an offer for *me*."

She'd been involved in many negotiations, but she'd never been involved in one as unusual as this one. "You know as well as I do that it's not an offer for your soul. It's an offer for what you can do, your abilities and talents. You are the heart of this company and your Young Guns in the other room, talented though they obviously are, are marching to your beat."

"How very poetic."

"And true. Don't try to twist this into something it isn't, Rio. Companies hire people every day of the week."

"I'm not looking for work."

She wanted to strangle him. Instead, she cleared her throat. "Maybe I haven't been clear on that point. You wouldn't be just another employee. DI would give you a great deal of autonomy. You would still be *head* of your own company."

"I'm already head of it. And if I accepted your offer, it wouldn't be *my* company anymore—it would be yours."

She leaned forward, picked up the piece of paper, and gestured with it. "For a sum that would make you *rich*."

He made a dismissive gesture. "I've already made quite a bit of money, Yasmine. True, what I've made is not even a drop in the bucket compared to your megamillions, but, hey, it's a living."

She had the feeling he was now offering arguments not only to be difficult but to see what she'd say next. She thought again of strangling him, but decided it would be more prudent to just shake him. Except to do that, she'd have to grasp his shoulders, feel the heat from his body, feel the strength in the tendons and sinews beneath his skin, perhaps even run the risk of feeling a small amount of desire for him. Warmth tingled in her fingertips and crept up her neck to her face. She was astounded by her reaction. "You're an impossible man to deal with, Rio Thornton."

"And you're a very beautiful woman, Yasmine Damaron."

She'd heard it before, many times and said in

many different ways, but hearing Rio say it in his quiet, slow drawl and in a tone surprisingly devoid of argument and innuendo made her pulse quicken. It meant he was finally seeing her as a woman. It shouldn't matter to her, but it did—a revelation she'd think about later. Actually, she'd have a great many things to think about later.

She opened the piece of paper and held it up to him at eye level so he couldn't fail to see it. "This amount is a fortune to anyone, Rio, even to me." His gaze remained steady on her, but her hand didn't waver. She waited until he finally glanced at the amount, then dropped the paper on the desk and relaxed back in her chair. "Well?"

"You're right, it's a fortune."

"Yes, it is." She felt somewhat mollified. "In addition to that amount for yourself, you'd have the considerable resources of Damaron International to back whatever new idea or venture you'd want to develop."

He tilted his head to one side and looked at her. "You present an enticing package, Yasmine."

He was talking about the offer, but she also knew he was back to making sexual innuendos. She thought of calling him on it, but then decided she'd rather not give him the satisfaction of knowing he was getting to her. She also thought about leaving, but again, she knew it was what he wanted.

Though he probably didn't realize it, in the end he'd accomplished the exact opposite of what she believed he'd intended. Instead of repelling her and running her off, he'd fascinated her, challenged her, and strengthened her resolve to close the deal. "There's much more to the offer besides the cash, of course. There are stock options and—"

"I'm sure there's more, but I *repeat*—my company is not for sale, not for any terms."

She believed that was the way he felt then. She also believed she could get him to change his mind. Some people might think it foolish of her to be so sure of her success at this stage, but DI always got what they wanted, and they *really* wanted Thornton Software. Rio's company was the crucial part, the linchpin, of a whole package that she and her cousin Wyatt were currently working on together. "Everything is for sale. It's just a matter of agreeing to the right terms."

A smile touched his lips, the first hint of humor he'd shown in a while. "Tell me the truth, Yasmine. Those words are engraved on your family crest, aren't they?"

"We don't have a family crest."

His smile eased away. "But you'd have one if you wanted one, wouldn't you?"

"Rio—"

"I have another question."

This time she knew enough to be wary. "What is it?"

"Will you lose anything due to the fact that I've turned that amount down?"

"I beg your pardon?"

"Will you lose anything financially or emotionally?"

She exhaled a long, slow breath. "I know you're expecting my answer to be that I will lose nothing, but it's not that simple. No, my world will not end if the deal doesn't go through. No, Damaron International will not crumble. But acquiring your company is very important to DI for quite a few reasons."

He stared at her for several moments, his expression serious and considering, then abruptly he surged to his feet. "Go home, Yasmine. There's nothing here for you to buy."

It took her a moment to realize that she was being dismissed, but then she realized there was nothing else she could do but stand and hold out her hand to him. "We'll see each other again, Rio." It was the correct business response, almost automatic with her, and best of all, she reflected, it gave no indication of her shock over his abrupt dismissal of her.

He took her hand, but he didn't shake it, nor did he release it. "And how do you figure that?"

"For one thing, I'll be in the area at least another week. For another, I'm very determined and I don't give up easily."

"I'm not at all surprised," he said quietly. He lifted her hand to his lips and pressed a kiss to its back.

She was stunned, a little irritated, and undeniably physically shaken. The kiss felt warm and slightly moist, and it seemed to her that his lips stayed on her skin for a long time. It also seemed to her that once he ended the kiss, he straightened away from her much too quickly.

"It's been incredibly interesting meeting you, Yasmine, but, I assure you, my decision is definite." He moved past her to the door and opened it.

She stared at him, searching for some sign of what he was feeling. She wished that he'd been joking around with her, but he was serious—about refusing her offer and about wanting her to leave.

In an incredibly short amount of time he had managed to capture her interest, make her heart do and feel strange things, make her mind take wild, fanciful flights, and completely bewilder her. Yet he wanted her gone as if she were no more important to him than a door-to-door salesman.

The music still blared, she absently noticed, but the air was clear of flying missiles and the video arcade games were quiet. Everyone was working, though a couple of them glanced curiously over at her.

With the imprint of his lips still warm on her hand, she looked at him one more time. "Nothing is ever definite, Rio."

"*Damn.*" Expelling a heavy breath, Rio closed his eyes and lightly rubbed the lids. He really had forgotten the appointment. When he'd learned the week before that someone from Damaron International wanted to drop by, he'd regarded it as more of a nuisance than a big deal. He'd always figured that sooner or later the Damarons would get curious enough about him, or annoyed enough with him, to send someone to check him and his operation out. Under normal circumstances, they weren't a threat to him, not in any important way. But then, he definitely hadn't expected a Damaron like Yasmine to show up.

Anyone else he could have handled, but Yasmine . . .

She was all golden—her skin, her eyes, her hair, her ribbons. Hell, he could have gotten a retina burn just looking at her.

To make matters worse, she'd been too coolly assured, and she'd gotten to him badly. He hadn't handled the meeting well at all.

As soon as he'd realized her purpose for coming, he should have shown her to the door as he would have anyone else with the same purpose. But he hadn't been able to.

He hadn't been able to stop looking at her. He hadn't been able to stop himself from giving her a hard time and making double entendres and personal remarks. He hadn't been able to stop himself from reaching for her hand and brushing his lips across its back to feel the softness of her skin and the sweetness of her taste.

And he couldn't explain any of it.

His only consolation was that he was almost sure he'd gotten to her and that she'd been affected by him every bit as much as he'd been affected by her. But it was small consolation. . . .

Damn her anyway, waltzing into his office with her golden eyes and hair and ribbons and offer of millions.

If she were anyone else . . . had any other last name besides Damaron . . .

But she wasn't, didn't. And as it was, she couldn't have come at a worse time.

TWO

Bluebonnets and Indian paintbrush swayed in the green meadow before the spring breeze. The gold satin bow at the end of Yasmine's braid fluttered, its ends caressing her bare back. When she'd returned from Thornton Software, she'd changed into a halter top and a pair of shorts, but she scarcely noticed the feel of the ribbon against her skin.

"So what do you think?" she asked, glancing over her shoulder at Rachel McLain, her best friend since their schooldays. Rachel, six months pregnant with her first child, was ensconced amid cushions and pillows in a lounge chair, her feet propped on an overstuffed ottoman, her knitting in her lap. They were on a flagstone patio situated halfway between Rachel's new brick-and-glass house on the hill above and Lake Travis below. The branches of a majestic oak sheltered them from the late afternoon sun.

"I think Rio turned you down. I also think I *told* you he would." Rachel held up the pink baby's blanket she was knitting, to judge its length.

"I just hate it when you say *I told you so.*"

Rachel's heart-shaped face lit with mischief. "I know."

Yasmine turned to her. "You know what really got to me about him?"

"The fact that he didn't see you as a woman?"

"That *was* a small bother," she conceded. "Things changed eventually, but, at least at first, he saw me only as part of Damaron International."

Rachel resumed her knitting. "Which, of course, you are."

"That's only one part of me."

"Right—the part that had an appointment with him today."

Yasmine frowned, her gaze on Buster, Rachel's golden retriever, who was lying by the ottoman. "Rio had this irritating way of talking about business but making it sound disturbingly personal."

"You're confirming what I've always suspected, which is that Rio is an *extremely* interesting man."

"He's an *impossible* man."

Rachel nodded. "Most interesting men are, sweetie."

"No, no, you don't understand—we're talking *majorly* impossible." Brooding, she folded her arms beneath her breasts. "A perfect example is the fact that he kissed my hand. I mean, tell me *that* isn't weird. If you'd seen our meeting, the way he acted, heard the things he said . . ." Much to her annoyance, she ran out of words. "Well, let's just say it was the last thing in the world I expected him to do."

"Which, no doubt, was why he did it."

"Yeah, you're probably right." She stooped to pat Buster, who was the brother to her two golden retrievers, Davie and Dougie.

Rachel tugged more pink yarn from the basket beside her. "Yasmine, I don't understand. With all those larger-than-life men in your family, you've had more experience than most in dealing with the impossible of that gender, and I've never once seen you fazed by any of them. So why on earth are you letting Rio Thornton get to you like this?"

Pushing Rachel's feet over a little, Yasmine dropped down to the ottoman. "I don't know."

Rachel shook her head. "I don't either. Listen, just accept that he's impossible and get on with it. Either make him another offer or forget about him."

Yasmine frowned again. "Forget about him?"

"Why not?"

"Because he's like an itch I can't scratch—one giant, annoying *irritant*. For instance, he turned my offer down without even looking at it." She gestured incredulously. "*Who* in the world does something like that?"

"Rio obviously does," Rachel said wryly, then put her knitting down. "Look at it this way, sweetie. It didn't make sense to you that he kissed your hand, but then, none of the rest of the meeting made sense to you either, did it?"

"No, not really."

"Then there you are."

"And where exactly would that be?"

Rachel threw an amazed glance at her friend. "I honestly can't get over this. I've never seen much of anything ever throw you. This really makes me wish Brent and I knew Rio better."

"I wish you did too, then maybe you could give me some guidance."

"Like I told you before, Brent and I know him only casually through the health club. We've never actually socialized with him."

Yasmine reached for her braid and the calming feel of the satin ribbon. "I had to literally hold the offer in front of his nose to get him to look at it. How in heaven's name can a man do business like that?"

Rachel grinned. "I don't know, but he must be doing something right, or you wouldn't be so hot for him."

"Hot for his *company*. His *company*."

Rachel's expression turned innocent. "Of course that's what I meant."

Yasmine sighed. "I'm obsessing, aren't I?"

"To put it mildly."

"Sorry—I'll do better." With a rueful grin, she reached over and squeezed her friend's hand. She'd flown in from the East Coast the night before and they really hadn't had a chance yet to visit. "It's so good to see you."

"Likewise," Rachel said, her smile lovely. "I've been counting the days until you could get here."

Since they'd graduated from college and gone their separate ways, they'd made it a practice to see each other twice a year, sometimes meeting in Europe or the Caribbean. But this year Rachel's pregnancy had made her reluctant to travel too far from home, so Yasmine had come to her. She nodded toward the baby blanket. "What's with the pink? Have you found out you're having a girl?"

Rachel slanted her a knowing glance. "I told you the last time we talked that Brent and I want to find out the sex of our baby the old-fashioned way, in the delivery room."

"I thought maybe you'd come to your senses." Yasmine swept her hand through the air. "It'd be so much simpler all the way around to go ahead and find out beforehand. That way you'd know what colors to do the nursery in, what clothes to buy, what—"

"We haven't changed our minds, Yaz."

"But why? You're going to find out in three months anyway, so what possible difference could it make to find out now?"

"I realize that patience is a concept you have no working knowledge of," Rachel said wryly, "but for my sake and in this instance *try* to come to terms with it."

Yasmine flipped her braid behind her shoulder.

"All I'm saying is that it would be more practical to find out ahead of time whether you're going to have a boy or a girl."

"The sex of one's unborn child is one of life's sweetest mysteries. Brent and I want to savor the mystery for a little while longer."

"I *hate* mysteries."

Rachel laughed. "I know."

Yasmine surged to her feet and walked to the edge of the flagstone patio. Before her, a breathtaking blanket of blue and red wildflowers covered the gently rolling green meadow. In the distance, the sun hung low on the horizon and glinted orange off the lake. Soon Brent would be home and it would be time for them to go up to the house for dinner.

Where would Rio eat tonight? she wondered, her mind effortlessly wandering back to him. Whom would he go home to? Glancing down, she saw her hands clenched together and pulled them apart. She could feel the breeze cooling her skin, but it was doing nothing for her nerves.

She tore her thoughts away from him and looked back at Rachel. It was much easier on her nervous system to focus on the baby. "So if you don't know whether you're having a boy or a girl, why the pink yarn for the blanket?"

"Because today I think I'm having a girl."

"Then—"

"I have a blue blanket started in my bedroom."

Yasmine studied her friend, then grinned. "It

should be illegal to look as serene as you do right now, Rach."

"Thank you."

She strolled back to her seat on the ottoman. Expectantly, Buster lifted his head, obviously hoping for attention, and she obliged. "You know, Rach, as your child's godmother, I have a great many important duties. In fact, there are a lot of things I could be doing as we speak. What do you think? Would your doctor tell *me* what you're having? I'd keep the information secret, of course, but the information would certainly help me out no end."

"Not a chance."

Rachel vetoed the idea without dropping a stitch or raising an eyebrow, and Yasmine knew she'd probably been expecting it. "I could always hack into your doctor's computer system," she said in half warning, half jest.

With a merry laugh, Rachel put the pink blanket aside and rested a hand on the already-wide shelf of her stomach. "Now who's being impossible? One day you're going to learn that there are some things in life you simply can't control."

"The more I can control, the better I feel."

"Then for your own sake, you better forget Rio Thornton," Rachel said, her tone suddenly very serious, "because I don't think you're going to be able to control him in any way, shape, or form."

Outside of her family, Yasmine reflected, Rachel was one of the few people who knew why she hated surprises so much. It had started the day her brother, Lion, had come to fetch her from Rachel's house, where she'd been playing. Once he'd gotten her home, he'd told her that their parents had been killed in a plane crash—murdered by a business enemy who had sabotaged their plane by planting a bomb aboard. It had taken her a long time to recover from the shock. She'd learned to cope by striving to always be prepared and in control of any situation. She even hated surprise parties.

For several moments Yasmine tried to concentrate on the simple act of scratching the blissful Buster, but it didn't work.

"So, Rach, what do you think?"

"About what?"

"About Rio Thornton having a girlfriend. He probably does, don't you think? I mean, even though he made several sexual innuendos, it was more insulting than serious, so it only makes sense that he does. Have you ever seen him with a woman?"

Rachel grinned at her, then looked behind her, and suddenly Buster scrambled to his feet and took off in the same direction. Yasmine glanced over her shoulder to see Brent walking down the hill from the house.

Brent, a tall, handsome Texan, paused to greet a joyous Buster. Rachel had met Brent when she'd flown to Austin to visit an aunt. The next time Rachel had left Texas was to go on her honeymoon.

"You two look comfortable," he said, walking over to them.

"We are," Yasmine said with a welcoming smile.

Brent bent to press a light kiss to his wife's lips. "How are you, sweetheart?"

"Wonderful, just wonderful. In fact, now that Yasmine is here, I couldn't be better."

Straightening, Brent looked over at Yasmine with a big, broad grin. "So how did your meeting with Rio go this afternoon?"

Yasmine rolled her eyes. "Don't get me started."

Rachel laughed. "Come on, Yasmine. You know you're going to tell him everything."

"She certainly is," Brent said. "Over dinner. I've been sent to tell you two that it's ready."

"Wonderful, I'm *starved*." Rachel reached for his hand so he could help her out of the chair.

"Starved?" Yasmine pushed off the ottoman and looked at her friend in amazement. "You just ate almost an entire plate of crackers, cheese, and fruit not thirty minutes ago."

Brent laughed. "These days, she eats every fifteen minutes."

Rachel made a face at him. "Yeah, and look how *huge* I am."

"All I've noticed is how beautiful you are," he replied.

Yasmine looked on with a smile. The thing

she'd always liked best about Brent was how completely in love he was with Rachel.

He gathered Rachel under one arm and Yasmine under the other and started toward the house. Buster happily gamboled along beside them. "By the way," Brent said casually, "did I mention to you two that I had my secretary send Rio an invitation to our party on Saturday?"

Rachel turned wide, astonished eyes on him. "You did?"

Yasmine looked at him in horror. "You *didn't*."

Rio felt a familiar touch on his shoulder, then heard the equally familiar voice of Penny. "We're getting up a group to go out to dinner, and we're thinking Italian. Come with us."

Rio glanced over at his assistant, who had perched on his desk. Her flashing purple nails matched the painted streak in her hair, which in turn matched the micro-miniskirt and the midriff-baring T-shirt she wore. She looked as if she did nothing more than club-hop up and down Austin's Sixth Street from dusk to dawn, checking out the latest bands. But the fact was, her superb competence in handling his company's day-to-day business freed Rio to do the work he loved. She was invaluable to him. "Is it already dinnertime?"

"And then some."

His gaze drifted back toward the computer screen. His usual focus had deserted him that afternoon. He didn't have a moment to waste, yet since Yasmine Damaron had shown up a few hours earlier he'd done nothing but waste time. "Just bring me something back—anything, I don't care."

"You're sure?"

"I'm sure."

She hopped off his desk, but then paused. "A break would do you good, Rio. You'd come back with a clearer head. Bobby and Jack are sacked out in the office, but everyone else is going out to eat. Are you sure you don't want to go?"

"I've got to stick with this, but I'm glad the others are going. They need a break."

"Oh, and you don't?"

He smiled. "Just bring me something back."

She shrugged. "Okay, then. Do you need anything before I leave?"

"No. Oh, *wait.*" Abruptly he swiveled his chair around so he could look at her. "There is one more thing."

"Sure—what?"

"Didn't you mention an invitation to a housewarming party for Rachel and Brent McLain a while back?"

She nodded. "A couple of weeks ago."

"What did you do with it?"

"I sent your regrets just like you told me. It's the exact same thing you always tell me to do with any invitation." Her expression turned curious. "Why do you ask?"

"Oh . . . no reason, really." He leaned back in

his chair and briefly pressed his thumb and forefinger against his eyelids. "Yasmine Damaron is staying with them."

"Oh, really?" Penny grinned. "She was amazing-looking, wasn't she?"

Amazing didn't even begin to describe Yasmine, he reflected grimly. "Do you remember when the party is?"

"Tomorrow evening—Saturday. Do you want me to call them and say you've changed your mind?"

"No." He shook his head firmly. "I don't have the time to spare, you know that."

She gazed down at her iridescent purple nails. "I wish you'd change your mind. For one thing, it looks like I have a date for that particular little shindig, which isn't the sort of thing I usually attend."

"Oh, yeah?"

"Yeah, and . . ."

Letting Penny's words flow over him, he rested his head against the back of his chair. Lord, he was tired. But he didn't think it was the kind of tired that a good night's sleep was going to cure. He'd worked night and day for the last couple of weeks, with only the occasional nap to keep him going. With the added frustration of a stymied, nearly overdue project, his mind had just about shut down.

There was only one project he wanted to work on, one project that had his heart and soul—

Tsunami. He'd picked the name himself for the new and revolutionary operating system he'd created.

Tsunami meant a great sea wave—a tidal wave. No one outside his company knew about it yet, but when it was finished and out on the market, it would sweep over all the other competition, overwhelming them, right up to and including Bill Gates.

But first he had to make sure that all the bugs were out of it and then put the finishing touches on it. Once that was done, its launch would need to be handled just right and in a major way. To do all that would take a great deal of money—money he didn't have.

The money was the reason he'd fought the Damarons over the Borggeo-Wagner contract. He'd needed the contract's up-front money to keep him afloat a little while longer until Tsunami could be completed, but things hadn't gone as he'd planned.

The Borggeo-Wagner contract was for an application—complicated, yes, but something that normally should be relatively easy for him to do. Unfortunately his mind had been on Tsunami for so long, he hadn't known how to stop thinking about it. Even when he'd turned it over to his crew to begin running tests, it had proved too hard for him to let go and he'd kept working on it himself.

When he finally turned his attention to the Borggeo-Wagner application, he ran smack into a wall. Now the contract deadline was almost up and the up-front money was nearly gone, and if he didn't figure out the problem immediately, he was going to lose everything.

Then Yasmine Damaron showed up, distracting him even further and offering him enough money so he'd never again have to worry about where the money for his next project would come from. In fact, he'd never have to worry about money again. He'd have to be dead not to be just a little tempted, but he'd never sell his company.

Unfortunately, she'd caught him at an extremely vulnerable time. If she were to get wind of his financial difficulties and let the word out, the industrywide confidence in his company he'd worked so hard to build would collapse. Borggeo-Wagner might even pull the contract from him and demand their money back. That would be nothing short of a disaster for him.

"You're not listening to me, Rio."

"Sure I am," he said, blinking Penny back in focus. "So who's the lucky guy now?"

"I just told you—Michael."

"Michael?" Penny changed guys more often than she changed the color of her nail polish, which in some cases was twice a week.

She rolled her eyes. "You *weren't* listening. I met him last week at the grocery store. He's just moved into the area because—*ta-da*—he's taken a position at Brent McLain's law firm."

Rio nodded. "That's a good firm."

"Yeah, and he's a nice guy. But I won't go to the party if you need me. I told Michael my plans had to stay flexible."

"I'll bet he loved that."

She shrugged. "He'll have to understand or else get another date."

He grinned wearily. "Go to the party and have a great time. Ditto dinner tonight."

"We won't be gone long."

"Take your time." He swung back around to face the desk, but instead of seeing the familiar sight of his computer screen and the problem that was giving him fits, he saw the exotic, heart-stopping face of Yasmine Damaron.

He knew the McLains only casually, but what he knew of them he liked. He didn't go to the health club on a regular schedule, but he'd run into the couple quite a few times there. In fact he and Brent had played a few pickup handball games that he'd enjoyed. Still, the acquaintanceship wasn't enough to warrant the invitation. No, he was certain his invitation had been sent because they knew their houseguest, Yasmine Damaron, had hoped to do business with him.

Not that it mattered what their reason had been. He rarely went to social events, preferring smaller intimate gatherings of people he knew well, and Yasmine's guaranteed attendance at this particular party was an additional reason he would not be there.

He was right in the middle of one of the most

important projects in his life and at the moment *nothing* was going right. He didn't have the time or the interest to go to a party. Furthermore, he could think of no reason he should ever see Yasmine Damaron again and a lot of reasons why he shouldn't.

"Rio," Brent said, hurrying toward him with an outstretched hand. "What a *nice* surprise. We weren't expecting you this evening."

"My evening unexpectedly opened up." Rio reflected wryly that his decision to come was even more of a shock to him than it was to Brent. "I hope it's all right that I showed up without calling."

"Are you kidding?" Brent asked jovially. "It's *more* than okay. As a matter of fact, Rachel and I would have been offended if you hadn't. Come with me and let's get you something to drink. The best margaritas in the state are being made and served here tonight."

"A soft drink will be fine," Rio said, following his host.

"When are you going to give me another chance to get beaten at handball?"

"Soon," he said with a smile. They were on the McLains' expansive back terrace, where the party was in full swing, and Brent was headed toward the far side, where Rio could see a bar had been set up. Farther along was a buffet, where waiters were serving wonderful-smelling barbecue with an amazing array of side dishes. The crowd was festive, the music lively, but he didn't see Yasmine anywhere.

As they made their way through the crowd, Brent greeted his guests with a smile, a pat on the back, or a friendly word. Rio didn't recognize any of the partygoers. Then again, he hadn't expected to. An impulse had driven him there tonight to see one person, and even if the journey across the terrace had taken hours instead of minutes, he doubted he would have had time to make sense out of why he had come.

He wanted to see Yasmine again—that much was crystal clear—but he wasn't certain why or what he would do once he saw her. He must be more tired than even he knew.

When they reached the bar, Brent turned to double-check with him. "Are you sure I can't talk you into a margarita?"

Rio nodded. "I'm positive. I'll be going back to work in a little while."

Brent laughed good-naturedly. "I've heard you were a workaholic, but all the same, I hope you won't want to leave too soon."

"Rio!" Rachel appeared beside them, her lovely face lit with pleasure, and looped her arm through her husband's. "What a *nice* surprise."

He grinned. "That's exactly what your husband said, and you're both being very kind."

"You're always welcome, Rio." She was wearing a loose-fitting pink silk shift that flowed over her stomach and down to her ankles. "I've missed seeing you these last few months, but I've just been too lazy to go to the health club."

He took a sip of the soft drink Brent had handed him, then used the glass to gesture to her stomach. "Looks as if you've had a good reason to be lazy."

"The very best," she said with a laugh. "Now, let's find Yasmine." She craned her neck to search the crowd. "She'll want to know you're here."

"That's not necessary—"

"Believe me, it definitely is. She'd be furious with me if I didn't find her." She looked back at him, her expression wry. "She's had a lot of interesting things to say about you."

Rio's mouth quirked. "I'll bet she has."

"Oh, there she is." She pointed toward the temporary dance floor that had been laid over the lawn just beyond the terrace. "She's dancing with . . ." She frowned. "Who *is* she dancing with, Brent?"

"Joel Snider. He's a new client of mine. He came to me because he needs help forming—"

Rio barely heard Brent's reply. Yasmine was all he could see, hear, and think of. She was wearing a bare little dress, its color somewhere between sea green and teal, its material shimmery. It had thin straps that crossed over her shoulders and plunged down to a low back and a short, full skirt that ended at her knees. Her hair fell loose around her shoulders and halfway down her smooth back. She looked even more dazzling than she had the day before in his office.

Heat stirred in his loins. Heaven help him, he wanted her.

The music changed to a slow, sensual samba, and her dancing partner gathered her closer to him. When she laughed up at the man, Rio felt something clutch in his gut.

Rachel grabbed his hand and pulled him along. "Let's go say hello."

"I don't want to disturb her," he said, his voice so stilted, he didn't recognize it. "She looks like she's having a good time."

"Well, sure—that's what parties are for."

Silently cursing himself, he gave up his token resistance. He'd tried to forget Yasmine and the fact that she was only twenty miles away, but he hadn't been able to. He'd tried to work, to focus on his problem at hand for the Borggeo-Wagner application, but he couldn't. He'd come tonight for the express purpose of seeing Yasmine again, and now that he was there, he was going to make the most of it.

Anything that involved risk had always attracted him. He loved the excitement and the thrill of a good gamble—the kind where a person played only against himself. At the present time, he was in the biggest gamble he'd ever undertaken, and everything he was as a man was wrapped up in it.

Seeing Yasmine again was also a kind of gamble. For him, she was the wrong woman at the wrong time, but she'd walked into his office, diverting him, distracting him—something that he hadn't thought possible. She'd been very sure of herself, and he'd enjoyed sparring with her, and that should have been that. Except after she'd left, he'd kept thinking about her.

By going to the party he was taking the risk that he could handle the excitement Yasmine offered without getting burnt. She wouldn't be in the area long. There would be no time to form a relationship, but even if it happened, it would be short and finite. Besides, Penny had been right when she'd said he needed to get away from work for a while. At any rate, what could it hurt?

"Yasmine, look who came after all," Rachel said, smiling broadly as they drew even with the dancing couple. "Isn't this a nice surprise?"

"Rio!" Yasmine stopped mid-step, causing her partner to stumble against her. "What are you doing here?"

With her extraordinary topaz eyes now trained on him, he felt a surge of exhilaration, as if some game had begun. "I was invited."

She dropped her hands from her partner. "But Brent told me that your office had called with your regrets."

"My plans changed."

Above and around them, tiny white lights twinkled in the boughs of the trees and cast bits of glimmer onto her skin and hair. Gold and diamonds sparkled and gleamed on her ears and around her wrist. She looked beautiful, regal, exotic, price-less—every inch a Damaron heiress to be looked at but not touched. Yet all he wanted to do was touch her.

Yasmine's dance partner glanced uncertainly from Rio to Yasmine and then back again. "Hello," he said, extending his hand toward Rio. "I'm Joel Snider."

"Rio Thornton." He couldn't tear his gaze from Yasmine to look at the man, much less shake his hand.

Joel's hand fell back to his side.

Rachel turned an enchanting smile on the poor man. "Hello, Joel. I'm Rachel McLain, Brent's wife. Would you please take pity on a poor preg-nant lady and dance with me?"

"Well, I—" He looked at Yasmine as if for help, but her gaze was locked with Rio's.

"Wonderful," Rachel said brightly, and unapol-ogetically taking the lead, she began to dance him away. "I want to hear all about you."

In an isolated pocket of space on the dance floor, he was at last alone with Yasmine. It was what he'd come for, yet now he felt uncertain. "Your friend Rachel has some smooth moves."

"She always has," she said, her tone cautious.

"And how many years is always?"

"In our case, since the fifth grade."

He slowly smiled, feeling more at ease. "I guess since the fifth grade would count as always." Gaz-ing down at her, he saw how her arms and shoulders gleamed so enticingly, and he remembered how soft and sweet the skin of her hand had been beneath his mouth. Remembering, seeing her again, made his throat go dry.

"What are you doing here, Rio?"

"I've already told you—my plans changed." She was looking at him as if she didn't believe him, and he didn't blame her at all. "Dance with me," he said, reaching for her and pulling her into his arms. This was what he'd been wanting since he'd first seen her, he realized—to have her in his arms, her body pressed against his, her sweet fragrance wafting around him, infusing itself in every breath he took.

She didn't resist, but she held her body stiff against him. "I don't understand. Did you change your mind about the offer?"

It was natural that she would think that, and he supposed he could pretend he'd come to discuss her offer further. But they were at a party and he saw no reason to mask his interest in her in the guise of business. "No. As I told you at the time, my decision on your offer is definite."

"People have been known to change their minds."

"I haven't." Even if he had, he wouldn't have been able to think of business with her in his arms. "Was the man you were dancing with a friend of yours?"

She shook her head. "I just met him, actually."

"Had you been dancing with him long?"

"No." Her brow knitted. "Why do you ask?"

"Because you looked perfectly relaxed in his arms," he drawled huskily, "and because you're incredibly tense in mine."

"It must be your imagination."

"No." He smoothed his hand up her bare back, following the line of her spine. "Tell me about the fifth grade. What were you like?"

He saw astonishment cross her face at the question, followed by a touch of humor.

"Freckles and braces."

He bent his head closer to her. "What about them?"

"I had them. I wore them."

He raised his head, his eyes glittering. "That's hard to believe."

"It's true."

He chuckled softly. "I'll take your word for it."

She was almost too surprised by Rio's sudden appearance to know what to say to him. Once again she hadn't been prepared for him. If the kiss on her hand in his office had stunned her, it was nothing compared to the almost paralyzing shock of being held in his arms against his hard body. She felt breathless, panicky, the way she normally felt when she was presented with something she hadn't been prepared for, but she could also feel heat gliding through her veins and she knew it was because of him.

"Rachel and Brent have a nice place here," he said quietly.

"Yes, they do. They picked out the land and started the design for the house right after they were married."

"It's nice when a plan becomes reality."

"Yes, it is." She had a feeling he hadn't been referring to the house, but it didn't seem important right then, when there were other, more intriguing things she was wondering about. Her curiosity won out over her panic, and her body began to gradually relax against his. "Did you come alone?"

Restlessly his fingers splayed open on her bare back, moved, flexed. "Yes."

The beat of the music changed, slowed, throbbed in a different, even more sensual way. There were other couples on the dance floor, but she didn't really see them. Rio was swamping her senses, taking all her attention. "I guess your decision was too last-minute for you to call someone?"

"I guess so," he murmured.

What she'd meant to sound like a casual, offhand statement had come out sounding as if she were fishing for personal information, which was unfortunate, since that was exactly what she'd been doing. But his reply had been maddeningly vague. "Is there someone who'll be disappointed that you didn't invite her?"

"Not that I know of."

She was a longtime master of social situations. For years she'd given and attended parties with élan, but in this situation she felt as awkward as if she truly were back in the fifth grade. He danced with her unlike any other man ever had, swaying with her more than dancing and sometimes not moving at all, but he made her feel as if she were floating. He held her unlike any other man ever had, his strength surrounding her and making her wish he'd hold her closer. "You don't seem the type who would go to a party for the mere sake of social obligation."

"You're right," he said, his voice deep and caressing. "I'm not."

She nodded and licked her tongue over the sudden dryness of her lips. "So?"

"So, Yasmine," he said slowly, "there's no one in my life right now, and I came here tonight because I wanted to see you again."

He had given her the exact answer she'd wanted to hear, yet it still knocked the props right out from under her.

She could handle business any day of the week, but she had to finally admit to herself that with Rio it had been personal right from the start. Now what she needed to do was adjust her thinking—take into account the personal and at the same time accommodate her primary goal, which was to acquire his business. The key, she told herself, would be to keep the exchanges between them light. Mentally preparing herself so he wouldn't be able to swamp her, as he was doing at that very moment, would take a little time. The problem was, she knew time was something he wasn't going to give her.

He slowly smiled. "What? No more questions?"

"No, I don't think so."

He chuckled softly. "You look different in the moonlight."

Different in what way? She badly wanted to know, but she knew that his answer would bring her more trouble. Besides, asking would give him an edge over her, making it appear as if she cared what he thought.

"You do too," she said, eyeing the beautifully cut navy-and-gray sport jacket he was wearing, along with a neatly pressed navy T-shirt and stylish gray slacks. "You look more"—she searched for a word—"conventional."

He threw back his head and laughed. "No one has ever called me conventional before, but let me tell you, my mom would absolutely love you if she heard you say it."

"Your mom?" She suddenly realized there'd been no mention of his family in the research she'd done on him.

"She knows that I'd rather have a root canal than go shopping, so every year for my birthday and for Christmas, my mom gives me what she calls *dress* clothes. She says she wants me to have something decent to wear in case I have to go to a funeral."

"A *funeral*?"

He chuckled. "It's how my mom thinks."

"I see. Well, she has good taste in clothes."

"I'll tell her you said so. She'll be thrilled to hear that someone actually noticed her effort to see that I'm dressed properly for the occasion."

"Even if it isn't a funeral?"

"She'll still be thrilled."

His boyish grin did strange things to her pulse. "What about your dad?"

"What about him?" He tightened his arm around her waist and turned them.

"What does he give you?"

"The gifts have both their names, though Mom is the one who actually goes out and buys them."

"She sounds like a nice lady."

"She is."

"And does she worry about you?"

He shrugged. "Sure. Don't most moms worry about their kids? Why?"

"I just wondered if she knew how tired you are."

His head jerked back slightly as if he'd been surprised by her observation, but he quickly recovered.

"It's probably the moonlight," he said. "It doesn't become everyone, you know."

She knew it wasn't her place to tell him such things, but she couldn't seem to help herself. "It's more than the moonlight, Rio. You're obviously working much too hard."

"It's what I do at times."

"But why now? You should be just about through with the Borggeo-Wagner contract."

"That's right." Wariness flashed in his eyes and then was gone.

But she'd noticed. Why would he be wary now? Was it something about the contract? "So why are you working so hard?"

"I enjoy my work, Yasmine. Why all the questions?"

She wasn't certain, except the weariness and wariness she saw in him bothered her. They made her want to see that he ate a good meal and got a sufficient amount of rest. Odd, since she'd never had the urge to take care of a man before, but she knew she'd never act on the urge. First of all, she had the funny feeling that more was wrong with Rio than would be helped by rest and a good meal; in addition, she couldn't see Rio docilely accepting advice from her.

"Yasmine? Rio?" Brent said, breaking into her thoughts. She glanced around to see Brent standing beside her.

Rio brought their dancing to a halt. "Brent? Is anything wrong?"

"Nothing, and I'm sorry to bother you two, but, Yasmine, you've got a call back at the house. It's your cousin Wyatt."

"Oh." She nodded. "Thanks, Brent." She looked up at Rio and saw that his expression had closed, but there was nothing she could do about it just then. "I'm sorry, Rio, but I need to take this call."

"Of course."

He took a step away from her, and she felt as if he'd gone a mile. "Will you be here when I get back?"

"I'm not sure, but probably not."

"I shouldn't be long." She hoped it would prompt him to say he'd stay and wait for her. But he said nothing.

THREE

All the way back to the house, Yasmine worried that Rio would be gone when she returned. She shouldn't care and she didn't, not *too* much . . . except his wariness had now gained her full attention. It was because of her, she was certain—or something *about* her that was causing it—and she wanted to find out what it was. Besides, she had been enjoying learning more about him . . . and dancing with him . . . and . . .

"Damn," she whispered.

What it really all came down to, she reflected ruefully, was the fact that if the phone call had been from anyone other than a member of her family, she wouldn't have left Rio. That fact alone spoke volumes about her fascination with him.

In this case, however, Wyatt was not only her cousin, he was working directly with her on several business matters.

She took the call in her bedroom. "Hi, Wyatt."

"Hi, babe. Did I catch you at a bad time?"

She smiled. Could there ever be a *good* time with Rio Thornton? "No, not really. Rach and Brent are having a housewarming party tonight, but I'm glad to hear from you."

"A party? Hey, listen, I'm in Toronto for the night. If you want to go back to the party, you can give me a call in a couple of hours."

The guest bedroom she was staying in was at the back of the house, and she actually found herself taking the phone and walking to the window to gaze out, but there was no sign of Rio amid the party guests.

She returned to her perch on the edge of the bed. "No, let's talk now. As I said, I'm glad to hear from you." She was always glad to hear from Wyatt. His laid-back ways and his sleepy eyes covered a razor-sharp mind, and they'd always worked well together. Besides, hearing from him was providing her with a badly needed touchstone that grounded her to reality. "Did you get my fax?"

"Sure did. Thornton turned down your first offer."

She grimaced. "Not only that, he said in no uncertain terms that he wasn't interested in *any* offer."

"Well, we knew going in that Thornton was going to be a tough nut to crack."

"Yeah, but what I didn't know was exactly *how* tough he would be."

"That bad, huh?"

She grinned at the amusement she heard in his voice. "That bad."

"So what's next?"

She exhaled a quiet breath. "My original plan was to give him the weekend to mull over the original offer and to think about what that much money would mean to him and his company, then first thing Monday morning present him with a new offer."

"Your *original* plan? Something's changed?"

"Yeah, he unexpectedly showed up here at the party tonight."

Wyatt let out a low whistle. "No kidding?"

"No kidding," she said, her tone wry. There was much more she could tell Wyatt. She could tell him about the sensual desire that had gripped her when Rio had taken her into his arms, or she could tell him about the heat that flared inside her every time he slowly smiled at her. Wyatt would be understanding and offer advice. She, Wyatt, her brother, Lion, and the rest of her cousins were all used to talking things out with one another. They had learned early to lean on family members when they had problems.

But in this instance she felt a peculiar reticence to tell Wyatt something she didn't yet understand herself. If and when she figured it out, then maybe. But until then she would deal with it herself.

"Does Thornton want to talk about the offer?"

"No, he definitely does not."

"Then what's he doing there?"

Her gaze gravitated back to the window. "Like he said, he was invited to the party." He'd also said he'd come because of her, but that was another thing she wanted to keep private for the time being.

"Well, I guess a man can go to a party if he wants. So what's the new plan?"

Good question, she thought. Hard though it was to admit, even to herself, when Rio had taken her into his arms she'd forgotten all about business. "I'm playing it by ear."

"With a man like Thornton, that's probably the best way, but there's something you should know. I picked up a rumor today about him, a rumor so faint, I practically had to put on a hearing aid to hear it."

"A rumor about Rio?"

"That's right. The problem is, I don't know how much credence to give to it, since I couldn't confirm it. And believe me, I've tried."

She frowned. The Damaron network extended far and wide. Normally they could find out anything about anyone if it was out there to be found. "Okay, so what's the rumor?"

"That Thornton might be in a bit of financial difficulty and could be trying to get a loan."

"That's impossible." She shook her head. "We would have heard about it before now if he was. Besides, my research didn't turn up even a fragment of any kind of trouble."

"I agree with you, but at the same time, I don't

think we can afford to completely discount it. Thornton Software is a private, well-insulated company, and you know as well as I do that in that kind of situation, you can hide a world of sins."

"Yeah, but if it were true, Rio would have shown at least a *hint* of interest in my offer, and he didn't."

"As I said, I couldn't confirm the rumor, and it was only a whisper. I might not have even heard it correctly, but I'll continue to check it out."

"Okay, and I'll see what I can do to check it out on this end."

"Good. One more thing—the deals on this end are all a go."

Yasmine sighed to herself. As they'd planned, Wyatt had been making deals based on the certainty that she'd be able to close the deal with Rio. It hadn't even occurred to her that she might fail. It still didn't, but she now knew it was going to be a little more complicated than she'd originally thought.

She mentally shrugged and told herself it would work out. "I'm glad to hear things are going well on your end, and I should have some good news to add to yours within a few days."

"Great. I'll talk to you then. In the meantime, if you need any help—"

She smiled. "I'll call, and in any event, I'll talk to you the first of next week."

"Talk to you then, sweetheart."

She hung up and stared down at the phone.

In her experience, money opened all doors, and she'd never been faced with a deal she couldn't close. Rio had proven difficult, but she had no plans to let Wyatt or her family down. With Thornton Software in their pockets, along with the companies Wyatt had lined up, the computer division of Damaron International would be in an excellent position to go into the twenty-first century completely independent and without having to depend on the whims, time schedules, and prices of vendors.

But first she had to come up with a deal that Rio Thornton couldn't refuse.

"Are you leaving?"

At the sound of Penny's familiar voice, Rio swung around. "I was thinking about it."

"How hard?" she asked.

"Not too hard."

"I'm glad to hear it. I saw you dancing with Yasmine Damaron. Did you run her off?"

"She went to take a phone call."

The last time Rio had seen Penny, her hair, outfit, and nails had all been purple. Now she was wearing a relatively sedate silver dress that matched her nails, and her brown hair, he noted, was completely free of paint and had been brushed until it shined. "You're looking very pretty tonight."

"Thank you." She gave a little curtsy. "I thought the occasion warranted a slightly different fashion statement." She eyed him up and down. "And apparently you had the same idea, because you're looking mighty extreme yourself."

"Thanks."

She threw a quick, appreciative glance around them. "This is some party, huh?"

"Some party," he agreed.

She looked back at him, her expression serious. "I'm glad you decided to come, Rio. You needed to get away from work in the worst way."

"So you've been telling me," he said. "Where's this new guy of yours?"

"Michael? When I saw you standing over here by yourself, I sent him off to get me a drink. I wanted to talk to you."

"About?" He scanned the crowd, wondering if Yasmine was through with her call yet. He also wondered at himself for wondering.

"Did you know that Tex Camden is here tonight?"

"Camden?" He shook his head. "No, I didn't."

"Yeah, well, it's amazing how many people you can miss when you spend all your time staring into a pair of topaz eyes." He sent her a dark look and she laughed, not the least bit intimidated. "Sorry. I couldn't resist."

"Next time, *try*."

"Okay, okay, getting back to Camden—have you talked to him yet?"

"I called him yesterday. He was *tickled pink*—his word choice, by the way—to hear from me and said that he's more than happy to look into the possibility of letting me have a loan." He paused. "Of course, there's just one *little* hitch. A loan for that amount of money has to go before the full board of directors, and a couple of them are out of town, one of them where he cannot be reached."

"Oh, great," she said in disgust.

"Yeah." He nodded. "Camden's going to check into a couple of things, but between you and me, it looks as if by the time they get back into town . . ." His voice trailed off. There was no need to say any more. Penny knew the situation almost as well as he did, though she was the *only* one who did.

From the beginning, he'd operated on a shoestring. At heart a wildcatter like his grandfather with a penchant for risk taking, he'd routinely cut things close. He'd kept that practice up in the last few years, using the extra money he was making to expand and heavily reinvest in the research-and-development part of his company. Everything had gone well until the Borggeo-Wagner contract. Still, he'd waited until practically the last minute to contact the bank, because he'd been so confident that the correct way to code the application would come to him.

But now, for the first time, he was very much afraid that he'd misjudged and cut things too closely and that this time he wouldn't be able to pull the rabbit out of the hat as he'd always done before.

He shook his head in self-disgust. "I shouldn't be here. I should have stayed the hell at work."

"No, Rio, you *shouldn't* have stayed at work."

He raked his fingers through his hair. "But if I just keep at it, sooner or later my mind is bound to click into gear."

Penny put her hand on his arm and her voice rang with concern. "It *will*, but only if you give yourself a break. Rio, you've been pushing yourself for so long, your mind has locked up. In the long run, taking tonight off or even a few days off will save you time, frustration, and money. You'll see."

He grinned in spite of himself. "Thank you, Dr. Penny, for your brilliant analysis of my situation."

"You'll get my bill. Now"—she scanned the crowd—"let me see if I can find Tex Camden. A little public relations never hurt anything. You can just mosey over to him and say hello."

"I don't do *mosey*, Penny."

"Which is the whole point." Her gaze on the crowd, she absently patted his arm. "You're normally so antisocial that he probably doesn't even know what you look like. Oh, wait, there he is."

"Where?" he said, half curious, half resigned.

"Over there." She pointed one silver nail. "See the rotund guy in the beige western-cut suit, the one with the white-haired lady wearing all those diamonds?"

He nodded. "Yes."

"That's him. Go over and have a little chat with

him. Maybe he's heard from that board member. At any rate, what can it hurt to be friendly?"

"Rio?" Yasmine's voice cut across their conversation.

He spun toward her. His body tensed. "Yasmine, I didn't see you there."

"I haven't been standing here long, just a few seconds. You two were so engrossed in your conversation, I was afraid to interrupt."

"You should have spoken up sooner," he said coolly.

Yasmine eyed him curiously. For whatever reason, his mood had changed while she'd been inside. She turned to Penny with a smile. "Hello. Nice to see you again."

"Likewise," Penny said pleasantly. "I've been telling Rio how happy I was to see him here tonight. He's been working way too hard and has been badly needing a diversion."

"Thank you, Penny," he said curtly. "Your date's probably looking for you. At any rate, surely he's gotten your drink by now."

Yasmine gazed up at him. "Do you need to go speak to someone?" She'd overheard Penny's description of a man, then had seen him when Penny had pointed toward him.

"No," Rio said firmly.

"Yes," Penny said almost as firmly.

"Penny, go find Mitchell, or whatever his name is." He reached for Yasmine's arm. "Come on, let's go for a walk."

"A walk?"

"Either that or go home with me." His tone, hard-edged and biting, made it clear he didn't care one way or the other.

She glanced at Penny, who gave her a nod of encouragement, but since she had no idea what Penny's nod meant, she went with what she wanted to do. "A walk sounds good," she said mildly, and taking the initiative, started off.

"My date's name is Michael, Rio," Penny called after him as he fell into step beside Yasmine.

"Whatever," he called back.

Yasmine had hoped she would find Rio still at the party when she returned from talking to Wyatt. On the other hand, she hadn't wanted to continue their dancing. Being in his arms clouded her thinking and made her body turn traitorous, heat, soften. His idea of a walk had seemed the perfect solution to her.

But as they proceeded across the lawn that slanted downward toward the meadow and the lake beyond, his cool silence continued. "Rio, is something wrong?"

"Not a thing."

She didn't believe him, but there was absolutely no reason he should confide in her. This was only the second time they'd seen each other. She wanted his company; he wasn't interested in selling it to her. Other than that, they had no relationship. Simple, yet somehow things had managed to become complicated between them. She quietly sighed.

A breeze had come up, blowing her skirt against her legs, her hair away from her face, and carrying the music along with them as they walked. Ribboning in and out of the wind's current, the music began to sound darker, more seductive.

Halfway down the sloping lawn, she noticed lanterns lighting the patio where she and Rachel had sat and chatted several times since she'd arrived. With a gesture of her hand she indicated the area. "Would you like to go over there?"

"Why not?"

The walk didn't seem to be improving his mood. It wasn't her responsibility to try to change his mood, but there was something she wanted to say to him. "I'm glad you didn't leave the party while I was gone."

"Penny caught me before I could."

"I'm still glad."

"Are you?" For the first time since they'd started their walk, he looked over at her.

He'd sounded a little surprised, she thought with relish. Finally it was her turn to catch him unaware.

"Why?"

"I don't really know, since you weren't exactly welcoming when I returned."

Several moments of silence passed before he finally spoke. "I'm sorry, Yasmine. My bad mood had nothing to do with you. And truthfully, I don't know whether I would have left the party even if Penny hadn't caught me."

Coming from him, that had been quite an admission, she reflected, and she decided to remain quiet to see if he'd give a reason for his bad mood. Then again, she should have known he wouldn't.

"Did you have a good talk with your cousin?"

"Yes, I did. He's in Toronto this evening, and he and I needed to touch base on a few matters."

"I'm sure you did." A smile touched his lips, and he seemed to be relaxing.

She found herself chuckling. "Yes, Rio, Wyatt and I *did* talk about you."

"I just bet you did." His smile stayed as they reached the terrace. After giving the chairs and tables a glance, he lazily surveyed her. "Do you want to sit down?"

She shook her head. "Not right now."

Stars hung in the clear black-velvet sky above them, and a three-quarter moon added a magical brilliance to the night, creating a shining path across the lake below them. The music from the party was still with them, its sound lower, its rhythm raw and sexual. She felt too restless to settle down in any one place.

"Are you and your cousin close?" he asked.

"I'm close to all my cousins, plus my brother."

"You have a brother?"

A sudden gust of breeze blew strands of her hair across her face. She tucked them behind her ear, very aware of his gaze on her movements.

"Yes. His name is Lion."

Rio made his way around the patio, giving the glider an absent push and the lanterns a cursory investigation. Obviously, she wasn't the only one who felt restless.

"You'll have to forgive me if I'm not up on the various branches of the Damaron family tree. All I know is that there are a lot of you."

"Thank goodness there are," she murmured. "We're all we have."

"The plane crash." He nodded, his smile instantly vanishing. "I *do* know about that."

Bringing up her family's tragedy was the last thing she'd intended or wanted, and she quickly spoke again, her aim to steer him in a slightly different direction. "Are you an only child?"

"That's correct." His eyes narrowed. "Whatever article you read on me must have been a good one, because I *never* talk about my family in interviews."

"Actually I read as many articles as I could get my hands on, which weren't that many, but none of them mentioned your family." She lightly clasped her hands together and rocked up and back on her toes. "You've given only a handful of interviews, and in one of the articles the reporter mentioned that you were cooperating only under protest."

He flashed a grin. "That's the way I do all of them."

"Why? I mean, if you hate interviews that much, why give them at all?"

He walked to the edge of the terrace and gazed in the direction of the lake, where moonbeams danced on the water's surface. "I do it for my father."

"Your father?"

He turned back to her, his expression sardonic. "From his viewpoint, articles in business journals make me seem more . . . *legitimate.*"

"You've *got* to be kidding," she said incredulously.

"Not even a little."

"Legitimate? Doesn't your father know how brilliant you are at what you do?"

"I suppose fathers have a different way of looking at their sons than at other people, a different yardstick by which they measure them."

"Rio, there's only one way you can be measured. You're a very successful man."

His lips quirked. "Thanks, but, you see, I don't get a paycheck on the first and the fifteenth of the month."

"A regular paycheck? *That's* his idea of successful?" Rio appeared surprised and a little gratified that she'd risen so quickly to his defense. More than likely she was overreacting, she thought. Still, she couldn't help but be truly indignant on his behalf.

He slowly walked toward her. "At age eighteen and fresh out of school, Dad went to work as a bookkeeper for a rock-solid paper goods company and continued in their employ until he turned sixty-five and they retired him with a gold watch. That was three years ago." He stepped closer to her. "*That's* his idea of being successful."

She gestured impatiently. "That's ridiculous. This is the nineties, for heaven's sake."

"Well, there's a little more to his thinking than what I'm willing to go into, but it doesn't matter." He reached out and touched her hair. "You're very good for my ego."

"There are very few men in the world who need their ego stroked less than you do, Rio, and they're all in my family. You're a very confident man."

He smiled down at her, and as always happened when he did that, heat flared inside her. A burst of laughter drifted down to them from the party. The leaves of the giant oak rustled above them. She could feel Rio's body heat reaching out to her and her pulse accelerating. "Maybe you should show your father my offer to buy your company. If *it* won't convince him that you're successful, then nothing will."

He gently pressed two fingers to her lips. "We've inadvertently strayed into dangerous territory."

His deep, husky voice sent a shudder of electricity through her. "What do you mean?"

"We're talking about business."

Strangely enough, she agreed with him. Tonight she didn't want to talk about business—a dangerous condition for her. She'd met him because of business. She had already planned to see him again on Monday because of business. She should be talking business with him right now, but the night was too lovely and she was enjoying being with him too much.

"Okay." She moistened her lips and carelessly licked the spot he'd touched, and received a sample of his taste. As casually as she could manage, she moved away from him. "I have a personal question for you."

"You can ask," he said, watching her, "but I won't promise you'll get an answer."

She glanced over at him. "You're a very guarded man."

"Not usually."

"Are you saying you're guarded only with me?"

His face was shadowed, his eyes enigmatic. "You're a very dangerous woman, Yasmine."

"How?"

"Look in the mirror sometime."

He'd chosen to give her a flip answer instead of the truth, but instinctively she knew that pursuing the truth would end up upsetting her, and tonight she didn't want to be upset.

"I think you'll find this a fairly easy question," she said, attempting to keep her tone light. "How did you get the name Rio? Is it your father's name?"

With a chuckle, he visibly relaxed. "No, it was from my paternal grandfather. The story goes that when he came to visit the hospital shortly after I was born, he discovered both my mother and father asleep, worn out from the night's effort of having me. So when the nurse came around asking questions for the birth certificate, he supplied the name of Rio, knowing full well my parents had already picked out the good, solid, respectable name of William."

"You mean you could have been called Will Thornton?" Laughing, she shook her head. "Somehow it doesn't have quite the same flair, does it? But why Rio?"

"My grandfather always said that some of the best times he ever had were spent camping out along the Rio Grande."

"That's a wonderful story," she said.

"And a true one."

With a couple of steps he was standing in front of her again, and he reached for her hand. She tried to keep her expression neutral and not react to his touch, but it wasn't an easy feat since her heart was pounding and her blood was racing.

"Have you ever been to the Rio Grande?" he asked.

"This is only the second time I've been to Texas. The first time was for Rachel's wedding."

"If you ever get the chance, you should go down there. Practically every turn of the bend is a different view. My grandfather saw to it that I went on lots of camping trips along the river with him during school holidays and summer vacations. He passed his love of the river on to me."

She spent several moments trying to envision

him as a young boy, sleeping under the stars and learning about nature and the moods of a river. She liked what she saw. "Even though you can't surf it?" she asked, her humor gentle.

"Even though I can't surf it," he said, agreeing with a grin.

"So what did your parents do when they woke up and found their son had been given a decidedly unconventional name?"

"Oh, I think it was a long while before either of them spoke to my grandfather. However, knowing him, I don't think it bothered him too much."

"He didn't care what people thought of him? Now I know where you get it."

"Let's talk about something else." With his free hand he stroked his fingers down her hair until he reached her shoulder. "I like your hair loose like this."

She pulled her head back, this time unable to stop herself from reacting. His touch had much too powerful an effect on her. "Thank you."

"I miss the ribbon though."

"The ribbon?" She wore ribbons more often than not, particularly when she plaited her hair to hold it away from her face, but she wasn't certain what about the ribbon could have attracted his attention.

"You kept fiddling with the ends." He picked up a strand of her hair from the side of her face and rubbed it between his thumb and fingers. "Like this."

She smiled self-consciously. "It's an old habit. Usually I'm not even aware that I'm doing it."

"It's a *diverting* habit."

"In what way?"

He didn't answer, but simply stood there gazing down at her, caressing her hair, and creating an aching heaviness in the lower part of her body.

"Rio?"

"It's a sensual gesture," he said softly, "and it's also a little-girl gesture. A man could go crazy trying to figure it out." He gently tugged on her hand, drawing her out of the lantern light and into the shadows of the spreading oak. Then almost leisurely he pulled her against him, lowered his head, and covered her mouth with his.

Passion exploded inside her and heat flared until it filled her. Dazed, dizzy, hungry, she reached out for his shoulders to steady her, to keep from falling, then slid her arms around his neck to draw him closer.

She wasn't surprised by his kiss or even by her reaction to it. From the moment he'd taken her into his arms on the dance floor, a part of her had known this time would come. If she thought about it a little longer, she'd probably conclude that this exact moment in time was the reason she'd been so eager for him to wait for her when she'd gone to take Wyatt's call. But she had no wish to think right now, only to feel.

His lips on hers were firm, demanding, his tongue against hers seductive and daring. The sounds of the party faded, the sensations of the night receded. She was aware only of him and the desire he was making her feel.

His arms were strong as they encircled her, his body warm and hard. He kissed her again and again, his hand roaming over her shoulders, her back, her breasts. She pressed herself against him, unable to get enough of his taste, his touch. She was very close to losing herself in him and his kiss.

She heard herself sigh, then make a soft sound of need. He murmured in response, though she had no idea what he said.

His kisses deepened; his tongue became more demanding, his touches more intimate. He stroked the strap of her dress off her shoulders, tugged the top down and closed his long-fingered hand over her breast.

She gasped at the new familiarity. His hands were very sure and knowledgeable, the night air against her skin gentle and warm. She quivered, moaned. . . .

"Come home with me," Rio said against her lips, his voice a hoarse whisper.

"What?" She could barely speak. She was too caught up in the world he had created for her, a world of heat and darkness and desire.

He lifted his head and raised a shaking hand to stroke her hair. "Come home with me, Yasmine," he said huskily. "Spend the night with me, make love with me."

There was a world of emotion in his statement,

and she could feel the same emotions vibrating in her. She wanted nothing more than to lie with him on rumpled sheets, wrap her legs and arms around him, and feel him deep inside her. But her mind was screaming the need for caution. It was much too soon. She never did things like this. It was crazy.

When she hesitated too long, his hands urgently gripped her shoulders and his dark eyes glittered intently. "Yasmine, we don't have much time. You'll be leaving in a few days. Come home with me *now*, while we still have the chance."

Her mind began slowly to clear. What he'd said bothered her, though she wasn't certain why. Her breasts still ached from his caresses, her lower body throbbed with the need he'd created in her. Trembling, she tugged up the bodice of her dress to cover herself. "While we still have the chance?"

His grip tightened. "That's right. Before you have to leave."

She took a step back from him as opposing feelings warred within her. "So what you've got in mind is a quickie fling for a few nights and then I'm gone? Out of sight, out of mind, right?"

"What?" His brow knitted in confusion. "I don't know what you're saying. Yasmine, you want me. I want you. What else is there?"

Everything he was saying was right, but why did it hurt her so much? Suddenly something clicked in her. "I'm that diversion you needed, right?"

"What?" he asked, bewildered. "*What* diversion?"

"You worked today, didn't you? And you probably planned to work tonight, but at the last minute you decided to come here instead. You needed a diversion, as Penny said, so on a whim you came looking for me."

His face began to darken. "I'm not sure what you're getting at, but it was *Penny* who said I needed a diversion, not me."

Her hands balled into fists at her sides. "But you did need one, didn't you? So you thought you'd just zip over here, pick me up, and take me home with you for a one-night stand."

Obviously trying to hold in his temper, he folded his arms across his chest, but every muscle in his body was tensed. "I honestly didn't think of it like that, Yasmine."

Bands of anger tightened around her until she felt as if she were choking. "But it's true, isn't it? When I came to your office, you listened to my offer for a short time, then firmly showed me the door. But tonight you sought me out and you told me yourself that it wasn't because of business."

"So what if I did? I don't get this at all, Yasmine. Not even a little. You had said you *weren't* going away, remember? You said you'd see me again."

"About *business*, damn you. Not about climbing into bed with you."

He gave her a dagger-cutting look and his voice

was stone. "Think about it, Yasmine. Face it. There was more going on between us that day than business. We were attracted as hell to each other."

Her anger climbed. She hurt and she wanted to lash out and make him hurt too. "Maybe so, but rational, sensible people don't go to bed with everyone they're attracted to. Or, at least, *I* don't."

Impatiently, he slashed a hand through the air. "Okay, this is enough. Listen to me, Yasmine, because this is real simple. I haven't been able to get you out of my mind since the day in my office, and I came tonight because I wanted to see you again. And true, once I got here I knew that I also wanted you, but I wasn't thinking of you as a diversion, okay? I didn't have anything planned. I didn't set out to deliberately seduce you. I wanted you, plain and simple, and so I asked you to come home with me."

"And you view me as nothing more than a diversion."

He looked away from her and raked a hand through his hair, and when he gazed at her again, anger blazed in his eyes. "Since that's obviously what you want me to say, then okay. Fine. You were a diversion, baby, and one *hell* of a diversion if I do say so myself. What man in his right mind *wouldn't* want you? I can't have been the first."

She felt as if he'd slapped her. No, he wasn't the first man who'd ever tried to have a meaningless affair with her. She'd easily handled those men, sometimes with grace and good humor, sometimes with sharp words. But none of them had ever made her as angry or had hurt her as Rio was doing now. Why? It made no sense. They were both telling the truth as they saw it. Why had she flown off the handle?

"You want me, Yasmine," he said, his voice softer now. "I want you. Why should we deny ourselves?"

She drew in a shaky breath and eyed him levelly. "I'm going to be honest with you, Rio. You're an amazing man. You just did an excellent job of nearly overwhelming me with your kisses, and yes, making me want you."

"Nearly?"

"And then I remembered I came here to do business with you, business which, I might add, *I* don't consider finished. I also remembered I respect myself too much to indulge in what would essentially be a one-night stand."

His voice and eyes hardened again. "As long as it's safe and mutually satisfying, which I guarantee it would be, what's wrong with a one-night stand?"

Mutually satisfying. Damn the man! His words conjured in her mind the emotions and images of her coming apart in his arms, and she couldn't handle it.

"And by the way," he added roughly. "Once we've had each other, I doubt very seriously if we'd be able to stop with just once, don't you? So you can scrap that quickie-fling crap."

"Good Lord, Rio. Is that supposed to make me

feel better? You might be the best thing since sliced bread—brilliant, sexy, innovative, whatever—but right now you're being a real jerk. But you know what? It's not really important, because in the end it all comes down to this: It doesn't matter what I think or don't think. It doesn't matter what you think or don't think. I'm *not* coming home with you."

He swore under his breath, then suddenly reached out for her. But for once she was quicker than he, stepping away before he could lay even a finger on her. If he touched her again, she thought, she'd either kill him or melt in his arms, and either option would get her in a whole lot of trouble. "Good night, Rio."

He stared at her in nerve-racking silence for what seemed like an eternity, his breathing harsh, his expression cold and hard. Then without a word he abruptly turned and left.

Something brushed against the back of her leg. "Buster?" She knelt and gathered him to her, more grateful than she could say for his undemanding presence and affection. Tears welled in her eyes, and with shaking fingers she brushed them away.

"Can you believe how incredibly stupid I am to shed even one tear over that wretched man?" she murmured to Buster.

Buster licked her cheek and wagged his tail, and the tears she'd been trying to hold back began to slide down her face.

FOUR

The office was uncharacteristically quiet, even for a Sunday, Rio reflected, staring blankly at his computer monitor. He'd have loved to blame the unusual quiet on his inability to focus, but he couldn't. The blame lay solely in what had happened the previous night between Yasmine and himself. Ever since, he'd been unsettled, agitated, confused, angry.

"Damn," he whispered as he stared at the phone. He wanted to call her, but even if she'd talk to him, he wasn't certain what he'd say to her. Yell at her, beg—he felt like doing both.

Last night he'd craved her so badly, he'd been in pain with it. Yet by asking her to come home with him, he'd hurt her, and he didn't exactly understand why. It was true they would have only a few days together, but what was wrong with enjoying each other while they could?

"Ah, hell," he muttered, thoroughly disgusted with himself. What was he doing thinking of Yasmine Damaron when he needed to be working?

He craned his neck and glanced into the big room off his office. Rock music was playing, but not at its usual high volume, and the caffeine was flowing. Five of his crew were there, all engrossed in their work. The rest of them, including a couple who had been there all night, had indicated they would be showing up within the next couple of hours.

They were the best of the best—young, bright, and completely dedicated to him and to the work they were doing—his Young Guns. Whatever he did, he didn't want to let them down.

He leaned back in his chair and rubbed his eyes. Like any truly successful risk taker, he'd always known and accepted that as quickly as a roll of the dice he might lose everything. This time, however, maybe for the first time, he wasn't willing to lose.

He believed in Tsunami, his blood was in Tsunami. When it hit the market, it was going to set the computer industry on its ear, leaving everyone else, including the giants of the industry, to play catch-up.

And he was *so* close to making it happen. All he needed was a little more time, a little more money. . . .

And then Yasmine Damaron had shown up in his life. She'd offered to buy his company for a fantastic sum that would solve a great many of his problems. She'd driven him crazy with her gorgeous body and her exotic golden beauty. She presented so damn many temptations, he was staggered by the count.

Giving a heavy sigh, he picked up a tennis ball and began bouncing it off the wall. "Hey," he shouted loud enough to be heard in the other room. "Somebody turn up the music." Within seconds, the music was booming, making it a little easier for him to think more clearly.

Before he'd taken off for the party, he should have given more thought as to why he was going. He should have delved more deeply into exactly what it was he wanted and what the consequences would be if he tried to take it. He also should have considered Yasmine's feelings.

One thing was certain: He'd definitely been thinking with a different part of his anatomy than his head. He supposed he'd been a jerk, just as she'd said. It would have been much better if he hadn't gone to the party at all.

Obviously the reasoning and logical part of his brain was occupied with Tsunami and the Borggeo-Wagner application, and because of it, he'd reacted to Yasmine on a very basic, primitive level. He'd wanted her. He'd gone after her. He'd tried to take her. No wonder she'd reacted so angrily.

His hand shot out to grab the phone, then just as quickly let it go. Hindsight was a great thing, but in this situation, pretty useless, since there would be no second chances. After all, why should there be?

Yasmine was the kind of woman who would be accustomed to being courted and pursued by rich, powerful men who showered her with fabulous jewels and gifts and most of all *time*. He didn't have any of those things.

And truthfully, amazingly, if he had last night to do all over again, he would probably do the same thing again, because, dammit, he *still* wanted her.

He hurled the tennis ball against the wall and caught it.

"Hey, Rio," Bobby said, "we need to talk to you for a sec."

He glanced around to see Bobby, Jessie, Pepper, Conner, and Jack crowded into the doorway. "Sure, come on in." He pulled out his top desk drawer, propped his feet up on it, and leaned back in his chair while they draped themselves around his office. "What's up?"

"Tsunami." Jessie flung himself onto his back on the carpeted floor and propped his legs against a wall. "We're finding all sorts of bugs."

Rio tensed and ran a hand through his hair. "But when I came in this morning and glanced over last night's test results, I didn't see anything major."

Pepper, her red hair piled haphazardly atop her head, shrugged. "So far there hasn't been. So far most of the bugs have been stuff we can handle."

"Most of them?" Rio asked cautiously.

Conner spoke up, his expression and tone showing dismay. "We've run into something extreme."

Bobby gestured animatedly, his long, dark hair swinging back and forth against his shoulders as he did. "Man, we were surfing along, there wasn't a cloud in the sky, everything was beautiful."

"And then," Jessie said, taking up the tale, "we got into the tube and *bam*"—he kicked one heel against the wall, demonstrating—"we wiped out."

Pepper threw up her hands. "The system crashed."

"And we were Jimmy Hoffa'ed—dead and buried," Jack added morosely.

Rio absently rubbed the side of his face and felt the stubble of an overnight's growth of beard. "What part were you in when you crashed?"

"UNIX compatibility testing," Conner said as Jessie swung his long legs off the wall, sat up, then folded them Indian-style.

Rio thought for a minute while his Young Guns sat silently around him, watching him. "Okay," he finally said. "Let's do it this way. Go back and look at module AL93. Start through it and see if you can find the problem there. If you can't, go to AR28."

"Gotcha," Pepper said, springing up from the floor.

"Will do," Jessie said, taking a little more time to get to his feet.

"If that doesn't work, give me a yell." Rio watched them as they all filed out of his office.

With any luck at all, they'd find the problem in one of the two sections he'd pointed out. He hoped they would. If they didn't . . .

He exhaled a long breath. It always came back to time and money. He just didn't have enough of either. And there was one more thing he didn't seem to have enough of lately, he thought grimly as he swung back to his computer.

Luck.

But then, he'd need more than luck to get through the afternoon without thinking about Yasmine.

Yasmine found Rachel in the sitting room just off her bedroom, lying on a white moiré chaise longue, her hand clutching her stomach. "What's the matter, Rach? You look pale." With a worried gaze on her friend, she sank into a nearby armchair.

Rachel groaned. "I don't think my little one likes barbecue. Or maybe it was the jalapeño dip he didn't care for. Or maybe I just made a pig of myself last night."

Yasmine chuckled. "Jeez, I can't imagine that. Just because I've occasionally seen you go through a gallon of ice cream at a time, I can't believe you'd eat too much."

Rachel threw a pillow at Yasmine. "Oh, shut up."

"I forgot to add that you usually top off the ice cream with a bag of chocolate cookies."

Rachel pointed a finger at her. "Just because you've got a flat stomach and I don't doesn't mean I haven't seen you go through your share of cookies and ice cream."

Yasmine chuckled. "What's with the worry about a flat stomach anyway? You'll have a baby in three months and I won't. It all evens out. In fact, if you ask me, you'll come out on top, because you'll have your baby *and* a flat stomach." She paused, wondering where she would be in three months and if Rio would even remember her. Probably not. "Wait a minute—you said he. Rach, you said *he*."

Rachel gestured weakly. "Today I think I'm having a boy."

"Why?"

"*He* played football in my stomach all night long."

"Are you sure *she* wasn't practicing ballet?"

"Trust me. There was nothing dainty about what was going on in my stomach last night. *He's* going to be a linebacker."

"Okay, I'll take your word for it. Do you need me to get you anything, like maybe a carton of ant-acid?"

"I've already had a carton, thank you. Sit with me for a while and let's gossip about last night. Maybe it'll take my mind off my unhappy stomach."

Yasmine pounded her fist into the pillow. "Great party."

"Uh-huh—it was very successful. Brent and I

were both very pleased. But let's get right to the point—our surprise party guest."

"Rio was a surprise all right," Yasmine said dryly. "But then, he's been nothing *but* a surprise ever since I met him. In fact, he's presented me with so many surprises that in an odd sort of way, I've started expecting them. It doesn't help me deal with him any better, you understand, but at least I don't panic."

"Well, *that's* good. So—last night? What happened to you two? I left you dancing with him, and then the next thing I knew, you both had disappeared."

Yasmine nodded. "I got a call from Wyatt, and when I came back, Rio was in a bad mood and wanted to go for a walk, so we went down to the patio and . . ."

Her voice trailed off as she remembered the things that had happened between them, things she'd been trying all night to forget. Instead of forgetting, though, the emotions and feelings that had passed between them had kept her tossing and turning for most of the night. And then when she'd finally fallen asleep, Rio had haunted her dreams.

"And *what?* Good grief, Yaz, don't stop there."

Yasmine grinned wryly at her friend. "I *did*, which was the problem."

"You did what?"

"I did stop. I let things get pretty hot and heavy, and then I stopped and said no when he asked me to go back to his house with him. And now I think I'm sorry—not for saying no, but because I think I probably *way* overreacted." She shook her head ruefully. "We had a hell of an argument, Rach, which *I* instigated. I just exploded all over him."

Rachel stared at her for several moments. "That's not like you."

Hugging the pillow to her, Yasmine rolled her eyes. "Tell me about it. I should have handled the situation much, much better."

Rachel leaned forward, her expression eager. "Okay, what happened? Exactly how hot and heavy are we talking?"

She shrugged. "Hot and heavy enough for him to ask me to spend the night with him . . ." She groaned. "That's when I flew off the handle. I took it as an insult and I felt very hurt."

"Just because he asked you to spend the night with him? Yaz, that's not like you either. More than that, it doesn't make sense."

Yasmine remembered thinking the same thing while it had all been happening. She'd known Rio such a short time, and no matter how attracted they were to each other, she had no intention of allowing anything serious to happen. She had much better sense than that. Therefore, she shouldn't have cared about his motives for wanting to make love with her as much as she had, and she definitely shouldn't have been as hurt as she'd been.

"You've always handled sexual come-ons very gracefully," Rachel said. "In fact, I've seen you turn men down so gently, they end up thinking it was *their* brilliant idea to back away."

Yasmine laughed and shook her head. "You're right. Maybe my body has been inhabited by aliens."

"And maybe you'd better tell me why you got so angry with him, and right now too. Jeez, Yasmine, a pregnant lady could go crazy with curiosity, waiting for you to fill in all the details."

She shrugged. "It just suddenly occurred to me that he was using me as a distraction, and I didn't like it."

Rachel's brow rose. "Using *you, Yasmine Damaron*, as a distraction? Well, that's certainly a first. So what did he say when you accused him of that?"

"He said he hadn't thought of it like that at all, and maybe he hadn't, but it was what he was doing anyway. So I told him no and he left."

"Wow." Rachel sat back and thoughtfully regarded her. "And you're okay with that?" She quickly waved her hand back and forth. "I don't mean the argument or the fact that you should have handled the situation better. I mean are you okay with your decision not to go home with him? Do you think you'll be able to leave here without feeling regret over that?"

"Regret?" Yasmine frowned. "That's a funny thing for you to ask."

"Well, you know what they say. At the end of

your life you don't regret what you did do, you regret what you didn't do."

Yasmine gazed at her broodingly. "I can't believe you're suggesting that—"

Her friend held up her hand. "Hey. I'm not suggesting anything. I'm only *asking* if you can leave here in a few days without any regrets about that particular decision."

"Yes, I can," she said firmly. "Once I have his company."

Her eyes glinting with amusement, Rachel rubbed her stomach. "Fine."

"Fine."

"Here you go, sweetheart," Brent said brightly, entering the room and bringing crackers and ginger ale with him. "This should make your tummy feel better."

Rachel groaned. "Let's hope so. I'd hate to be the first person in the history of the world to die of indigestion."

"Brent?" Yasmine said. "There was a man at the party last night, kind of heavyset, and—oh, yeah—he was wearing a beige western-cut suit. Do you know who I'm talking about?"

He straightened from having served Rachel. "You could be talking about quite a few people."

"He was with a white-haired lady who was wearing a conspicuous amount of diamonds."

"Mmmm . . . let me think for a minute."

Rachel looked up at her husband. "Sounds to me like she's talking about Tex Camden."

"Tex? You could be right." He glanced at Yasmine. "He's our local bank president."

"Bank president? How interesting."

Rachel shook her head. "Actually, Yaz, he's a very boring man."

"I meant it was interesting that he was a bank president. Brent? Do you happen to know if that's the bank where Rio does business?"

"I wouldn't have a clue. Why?"

"Oh, I'm just curious about something I overheard last night."

Rachel looked at her husband. "It appears that Yasmine attended a whole different party last night from the one you and I did."

Brent sat down on the edge of the chaise longue. "Now, *that* sounds interesting. Tell me about it."

Yasmine pushed to her feet. "I'll let Rach fill you in, because I know she will anyway." She shot her friend a dry glance. "Right now I need to see if I can get ahold of Wyatt."

"Give him our best," Rachel called after her.

"I will," she said, reflecting that she was also going to have Wyatt check into Tex Camden.

"Rio?"

"*Dad.*" Rio swung around to see his father standing in his office doorway. And immediately he tried to hide the fact that he wished his father had come at a more convenient time or at least had

called beforehand so that Rio could have been prepared. No matter what the circumstances, conver-
sations between the two of them were rarely
pleasant for Rio and always ended with the same
topic.

"What are you doing here?"

His dad, an older, slightly heavier, stooped ver-
sion of Rio, gestured with the casserole dish in his
hands. "Your mother sent me with some fried
chicken for you."

Rio grinned. "Mom's always afraid I'm going to
starve."

"You do look a little thin."

"I haven't lost or gained a pound in years, Dad.
Come on in."

Slowly, meticulously, the older man laid out the
meal on Rio's desk, occasionally throwing sideways
glances at him. "Your mother worries about you,
son. Just the other day she was saying how long it's
been since we've seen you. It's been at least a
month or two, she figured."

Rio wiped a tired hand over his face. He'd vis-
ited them less than a month ago, though he knew it
probably seemed like a much longer time to them.
"I'm sorry. I've been really busy, but I promise to
do better once I finish the contract I'm working on.
I do try to call Mom once a week or more."

"She appreciates that."

Rio sighed to himself. In his memory, he could
not remember his dad ever saying *he* was worried
about him or that *he* thought something about him.

It was always his mother. "Can you sit down for a while, Dad? Looks like Mom sent enough food for an army division or two."

"I ate earlier, but you go ahead and eat while it's still hot. I will stay, though, just for a couple of minutes." The elder Thornton seated himself, seemingly determined to watch his son eat every bite so he could report to his wife.

Eyeing his father, Rio bit into a drumstick. His father never seemed quite comfortable around him, especially after he'd left home and started his own company. They were diametrically opposite to each other in personality, but still, Rio often wished they could be closer, and he took full responsibility that they weren't. He worked too many hours to reach out to his dad often, but he was hoping once Tsunami was out on the market, he'd have more time for his folks. "How have you been, Dad?"

"I can't complain." His father paused. "But you should, son. You shouldn't have to be working on a Sunday."

Rio sighed inwardly. Here it came, the same conversation they had every time they were together. His father had worked all his life in the same nine-to-five job and he didn't understand or approve of his son's work habits.

As a young boy, his father had seen his own father go bust time after time in the Texas oil fields, and he had suffered accordingly. There'd never been enough money for food and clothes, they'd never stayed in one place and were always moving from oil field to oil field. The experience had forged his personality and made him the man he was. All of Rio's life his father had preached to him the importance of being conservative and having a steady, reliable job.

Unfortunately Rio possessed the same independent spirit that his flamboyant wildcatter grandfather had had, and it was the crux of the problem between him and his dad.

"If you had a good, stable forty-hour-a-week job, you wouldn't have to work long hours or weekends."

"A lot of people work weekends, Dad."

"But not a hundred-plus hours a week. And they don't eat and sleep in their office."

"It just depends on the kind of business they're in." It had always been important to Rio to prove to his dad that he could succeed doing what he loved and in his own way. But no matter how many successes he'd had in the past, or how successful he might become in the future, if he failed now, he'd never be able to convince his dad that what he was doing was right. The fact added to the pressure he was already feeling and weighed heavily on his heart. "Are you sure you wouldn't like some of this chicken, Dad? You know Mom makes the best fried chicken in the world."

Rio's father shook his head, drummed his fingers on the desk, then abruptly stopped. "Your mother doesn't think you've looked well the last few times we've seen you, son."

Funny, Rio reflected, he'd just been thinking the same thing about his dad, but hadn't known how to bring it up. To him, his father looked a little pale.

His father continued. "And your mother feels very strongly that working all these hours just isn't good for you."

"I'm fine, Dad."

"Now, son, hear me out."

He'd used that stern, father voice, Rio noted. The voice that no doubt he would flinch at no matter how old he grew. "What is it, Dad?"

"Your mother is concerned that you may be having some money problems."

Rio stilled. There was no way they could know that. They had to be guessing, but their insight astonished him.

"And if that *is* the case," his father said before Rio could gather his thoughts, "we don't want you to be too proud to come to us. We've got some savings in the bank—the rest, as you know, is invested, and then there's our monthly retirement checks. The point is, we've got plenty, and so your mother and I want to lend you as much as you need to ease your burden."

"Dad . . ." He was speechless and touched beyond measure. He knew how much they kept in their savings account, because they were scrupulous in keeping him informed of their affairs—in case, as they said, anything happened to them. Because of their modest lifestyle, his parents viewed their small savings as a great deal of money, but it was a drop in the bucket compared to what he needed.

Still they were willing to give it all to him because they wanted to help their boy. He couldn't remember his father ever telling him he loved him, but the gesture he'd just made spoke louder than any words ever could.

He felt like crying. "Thank you, Dad. Really. I appreciate your offer of help more than I can say, but I'm fine, and so is my company."

"Are you sure? Your mother doesn't want your pride to stand in the way. If you need it, it's there for you."

Because his father wasn't a demonstrative man, Rio had always reserved his hugs and kisses for his mother, and for the first time he was sorry about that. He reached over and covered his father's hand with his own. "Please tell Mom how much I love her . . . and you . . . and that I'll be giving you both a call in a day or two."

"All right, then," his father said a bit gruffly as he rose. The gruffness, Rio reflected, no doubt was covering the emotion of the moment. "But just remember it's there for you."

"Thank you, Dad, and take care of yourself."

Yasmine laid the novel over her lap and glanced at the clock on her bedside table. It was a little after eleven. She swiveled and gave the pillows behind her a few punches. She couldn't seem to get comfortable enough to read more than a few pages at a time, much less sleep. And why hadn't Wyatt called back yet?

With a groan she decided to give the book another try. Usually by this point in a mystery she would have figured out who the murderer was, but tonight she couldn't keep her mind on the plot. She'd called Wyatt early that morning and given him the information on Rio and Tex Camden. It was probably nothing, but she'd been too curious to simply let it go.

The phone rang and she jumped on it. "Wyatt?"

"The phone didn't even ring on this end," Wyatt replied with amusement. "You must have been sitting right beside it."

"Actually I'm lying in bed. It's late."

"I know, babe. Sorry to be so long in getting back to you, but it's almost impossible to find out anything on a Sunday."

"Yeah, I know that. I guess I'm just extra cranky tonight. Sorry."

"Are you okay? Do you need anything? What's wrong?" The questions and the concern shot out like bullets.

Yasmine smiled at Wyatt's protectiveness. "Everything's fine. Honest. I'm just in a funny mood." A mood called Rio, she thought ruefully. "So were you able to find out anything?"

"Not too much. I thought it best to speak only with the people I know I can trust explicitly. Still, in the end, I had to settle for a little expert speculation. The theory is that Thornton might have asked Camden for a loan and Camden had to put him off for an indefinite time."

"Might have? Theory?"

"I had to go with what I could get, babe, but expert speculation can often be as sound a base for information as anything else."

"If that's true, then Rio must be in trouble." She felt an ache near her heart for Rio. If it *were* true, he must be going through hell.

"Interesting, huh?"

"Yeah. And rather inexplicable since he turned my offer down."

"I'll say this for Thornton. If he is in trouble, he's managed to keep it to himself better than most. He's got an extremely tight lid on his company."

"You know, I just don't understand this, Wyatt. Rio's reputation is excellent. He's gotten contract after contract in the last few years, and there's never been a breath of trouble."

"That's true, but we know how low his bids have been, and we can safely speculate that he's undercapitalized. *He's* his main and most important asset. Any stumble on his part would be very hard on his cash flow."

It had been apparent to her from the first that Rio was tired. He'd also been wary of her, which now made sense. Her offer must be presenting him with a huge conflict. She was offering him what he needed most—money. Yet he would be the type of man who would want to keep the company as his own. She could understand that. But what she couldn't understand was his pride obscuring rationality.

The two of them were in a position to help each other. She had the money that would not only bail him out of his troubles, but make him comfortable for the rest of his life. And he had the company that would help hers become more independent and versatile.

Despite her concern for him, she felt a surge of excitement. Reason would kick in and he would change his mind about selling to her, because he was going to *have* to. And once he got a look at the offer she'd be taking to him the next day, he would have to give in and say yes. The deal was inevitable.

"I have more sources I can check out tomorrow," Wyatt said.

"No, don't do that. If this word gets out, by tomorrow afternoon Rio will have more offers on his doorstep than he'll know what to do with. We could be put into a bidding situation."

"That's true."

"My plan is to show up tomorrow at his office with a new offer, so let's wait and see how that goes."

"Do you have an appointment?"

"No, but I'm pretty sure his assistant will let me in."

"Good luck, sweetheart."

"Thanks." She grimaced. "I'll need it." Not with the deal—it now looked like a sure thing. What was completely *uncertain* was how they would react to each other after Saturday night.

FIVE

"Good morning, Rio."

Rio turned his head to see Yasmine, looking achingly beautiful. He scowled, even as his body tensed with need. "How in the hell did you get back here without my knowing?"

She pointed to the blinking light on his telephone. "I'm sure that's Penny telling you I'm on my way." She looked at the phone again. "Why isn't it ringing?"

He hit a key and his monitor went blank. Then he set the keyboard on top of the computer and swung his feet off the open drawer onto the floor. "I turned off the ringer."

"Why am I not surprised?" She shut his office door against the blaring rock music and took the chair at the side of his desk.

Her perfume wafted in his direction and he felt

a stirring in his loins. *Dammit*. Why did he have to be so glad to see her again?

She was wearing an elegantly tailored moss-green suit—Italian, no doubt, and more than likely couture, he reflected. Its skirt stopped above her knee, and when she crossed her long legs, the hem inched enticingly up her thigh. Her hair was in a single braid again, with a moss-green satin ribbon woven through the topaz strands and tied in a bow at the braid's end.

Her perfection made him keenly aware of his unshaven jaw and disordered hair. But he wasn't going to let her see his discomfort. His jeans had holes at the knees and his ankles were bare above his athletic shoes, but he nevertheless crossed one ankle over his knee and stared at her.

"I'm amazed to see you this morning," he said in a rough drawl. "You made it very clear Saturday night how you felt about me." He didn't go on to tell her how many times he'd picked up the phone the day before to call her, and how each time he'd hung up before he could.

"Saturday night was something personal between you and me, and I'm not here to discuss it. I'm hoping that we're both adult enough to put what happened behind us so that we can go forward with our business."

"Hey, that's me—adult," he said mockingly as a stab of disappointment pierced his chest. He would have welcomed a rehash, he realized. He'd heard her words, even understood them, but he was posi-

tive he hadn't fully comprehended the heart of
what had really been bothering her. His mind
wasn't clear where she was concerned, but he supposed it didn't really matter. The two of them
didn't belong together. Not now, not ever. Together he and Yasmine would be combustible.
Apart, they would both be much safer. "But I'd like
to remind you that you and I don't have any business between us."

She nodded. "Not yet."

Silently he cursed his situation. He couldn't
forget her, and he still wanted her, while she
wanted only one thing from him, and it was the one
thing in the world he couldn't make himself give
up. "So okay, Ms. Damaron, what's on your mind
this morning?"

One eyebrow arched. "Today it's Ms.
Damaron?"

"You're the one who wants to keep our acquain-
tance on a business level. Isn't that right?" Studying her thoughtfully, he leaned back in his chair
and steepled his fingers. "Or do I have that
wrong?"

She gazed at him coolly. "No, you don't, but I'd
rather you call me Yasmine."

"Thank you. That's very kind." He wondered
if, as she'd braided her hair that morning, she'd
remembered that he'd told her he liked her hair
loose. He didn't need the knowledge to gauge her
mood though. Her stiff business manner said it all.

Besides, he'd decided he liked her beribboned braid just as much as he liked her hair loose.

"I'm here today to make you another offer."

"Color me surprised."

"Rio—"

His lips curled sardonically. "You really don't take no for an answer, do you? I wonder what would have happened Saturday night if I'd had that same attitude?"

She went rigid and pale. "I've already told you—"

He held up a hand. "I know, I know. You didn't come here to talk about Saturday night." Exhaling a long breath, he briefly pressed his fingers against his lids. One of these days soon, he reflected vaguely, he was going to have to make an appointment with an eye doctor. The long hours at the computer were putting a terrific strain on his eyes. "All right, Yasmine, let's see it."

She blinked. "You mean you're actually going to look at it?"

He held out a hand toward her. Today he didn't feel like playing games. There'd been no breakthrough with the Borggeo-Wagner application, its deadline was two days away, and there'd been no new word from Tex Camden. To make matters worse, his assurances to his father yesterday apparently hadn't done the job, because he'd left looking very worried. Besides, he was vaguely curious to see what kind of offer Yasmine had come up with now.

As soon as she placed the offer in his hands, he

looked at it and his eyebrows rose. "Well, well, well, Yasmine. You've gone from offering a fortune to offering a fortune and *then* some. That must have been some number-crunching session you had when you came up with this figure."

She gazed at him without expression. "This is my second and final offer, Rio. I'd like you to consider very carefully all that DI is prepared to offer. If you do, you'll see—"

"No."

"That's your answer? Just like that? *No?*"

He nodded. "Just like that. No."

Total astonishment and disbelief crossed her face, and for several moments she simply stared at him. Finally she drew in a deep breath, and when she spoke it was quietly, calmly. "Rio, I really feel you made the wrong decision. Your answer was automatic and too fast. You need to think this through with more clarity."

"You think so, huh?" As he watched, she reached for her hair ribbon and idly rubbed the satin between her thumb and forefinger. She wasn't nearly as composed as she'd like him to believe.

"Yes, I do. Take more time to consider the offer, weigh the pros and cons. I'm confident you'll find a great many more positives than negatives. Beside the amount of money that would go to you personally, Thornton Software would have an enormous working budget. If you want, you could have the setup you have in the other room a hundred times over."

"The setup I have is all I need or want."

She drew in another deep breath. "The sky would be the limit for your research and development. You could promote your Young Guns, have each of them head a different project. You could focus the full power of your brilliance on projects that excite you rather than divide your attention among the more mundane ones. You could spend your time in creative thinking, where you excel, and leave the long hours to a *team*."

"I'm an individual, Yasmine," he said slowly, clearly. "I don't believe in working by committee, and I'd never allow a project of mine to be developed without my intense supervision."

She released the ribbon and sat forward. "I admire you, Rio. As small as your company is, you've gone up against some of the biggest in the industry, including DI, and more times than not you've walked away a winner. But I know it can't be as easy as you've made it look. I'm sure you've run into some problems along the way."

He slowly smiled at her, though he wasn't feeling particularly amused. "You just don't give up, do you? Then again, I have to say you did warn me."

"I warned you?"

"During your first visit here you said you're very determined and don't give up easily. I obviously should have paid more attention. If I had, then I could have taken precautions."

"Precautions?"

He shrugged. "I don't know, maybe changed

the locks, hired guards, put up a few bars on the windows. By the way, did you have an appointment today?"

"No, I didn't. You know, Rio, you're absolutely unique. People to whom I offer great amounts of money don't usually talk about barring me from their offices."

"I don't imagine people to whom you *don't* offer money talk about barring you either."

Her lips pressed into a thin line for a second, then relaxed again. "Rio, will you *please* think about this offer? No one in your position should summarily dismiss it. This is the chance of your lifetime."

He'd had enough. Enough of sitting there looking at her without reaching for her and kissing her senseless. Enough of her trying to buy him by throwing endless amounts of money at him, money that wouldn't take one dime from her own bank account. He pointed a finger at her. "Listen to me, Yasmine, and *hear* me. This is my company, my vision, and no matter what, it's going to stay *mine*."

"You're a stubborn man, Rio." Yasmine pushed herself up from the chair and restlessly circled the small office.

He leaned back in his chair, following her with a hard gaze. "And don't forget difficult."

"How could I?" she snapped, reaching for her ribbon. "Turn to the word *difficult* in the dictionary and there's your picture."

Seeing Rio again was harder than she'd even

imagined, she reflected grimly. She'd come determined to think and talk only of business, but one look into his dark gray eyes and everything about Saturday night had come rushing back to her. Business differences aside, it didn't seem right that two people who had kissed and touched as they had could react so coolly to each other the next time they met. But to give Rio his due, it was how she'd said she wanted it.

She'd been right to take that stance. She'd set the tone today and she needed to continue on with it.

And she had a decision to make. He'd turned down her second offer, and as a result she now needed to play what could very well be her trump card. Strangely, though, she was reluctant to do it. She could feel his gaze on her, the heat and anger of it, the impatience and the restraint of it, and deep inside her she felt an answering response. Totally inappropriate.

As she sat down, the two photographs on the wall behind the desk caught her attention. She remembered them from her first visit and deliberately seized on them as an excuse to stall. "Your family?" she asked.

Without dropping his gaze from her, he pointed to the two pictures. "The one on the left is of my grandfather, taken in West Texas in front of one of his oil wells that had just come in."

"Your grandfather was an oilman?"

His smile held only a small amount of humor.

"When the wells came in, he was an oilman, but when he hit mud and went bust, which was more often than not, he was just plain poor."

"I'm sorry to hear that."

"Don't be. He was the kind of man who got the most out of life no matter what his circumstances were. Rich or poor, he lived life to the fullest."

"He sounds remarkable. Is he the grandfather who named you?"

"He's the one."

"And the couple in the other picture?"

"My parents. The picture was taken about ten years ago." He paused. "Why are you still here, Yasmine? If it's because you think I'm going to change my mind, you can forget it."

Right, she thought. How could she have forgotten his dislike of idle pleasantries? Besides, there was no reason for her to put off the inevitable any longer. "I'm still here, Rio, because your refusal of both my offers doesn't make any sense to me."

"Of course it doesn't. You're an heiress who's accustomed to being able to buy anything you want."

"That's not true," she said quietly. "I couldn't buy back my parents' lives."

He didn't respond for a moment. "Point taken, and I'm sorry. But here's another point. My refusal of your offers doesn't have to make sense to you, only to me. And believe me when I say it makes perfect sense to me."

She hated this coolness between them, she

thought suddenly. Hated it with an intensity she wouldn't have thought possible. Unfortunately, there didn't seem to be anything she could do about it.

She'd probably mentioned her parents because unconsciously she'd been trying to get him to see her as a person instead of simply an heiress, but it hadn't worked. Who they were and what they were discussing had put them on opposing sides. And after the way Saturday night had ended between them, she was probably lucky he hadn't thrown her out on her ear.

She sat back in her chair and crossed her legs and tried not to be bothered when his gray-eyed gaze dropped to her thighs. It was all she could do to resist the impulse to give her skirt a quick tug downward. "Well see, Rio, that's the other thing. I don't understand why it makes sense to *you* to turn down the offer, especially when you're having problems."

"Excuse me?"

Had he tensed? She wasn't sure. She just wished she didn't feel this strange reluctance to bring up his rumored money problems. She also wished she didn't feel the inexplicable need to soften what she wanted to say. But she did and she was going to try.

"I understand and admire you for wanting to keep this company as your own, Rio. You obviously have the same independent, adventuresome spirit that your grandfather had and, in fact, that my grandfather had when he first started out. They both had an entrepreneurial zeal that made them willing to strike out into directions no one else had and—"

"And *your* grandfather became filthy rich and *mine* just became filthy." His eyes narrowed on her. "Cut out the flowers-and-candy crap, Yasmine. What is it you're dancing around?"

She shook her head ruefully. When was she going to learn? Any attempt to do anything but get straight to the point was doomed to failure with him. "All right, Rio, here it is. I'm still trying to understand why you won't take my offer if you need money so badly that you contacted a bank for a loan. Accepting our offer would solve all your problems."

"What?" he asked quietly, going very still.

Even though Rio had barely reacted, she now knew that the expert speculation had been right. "You're having financial difficulties, but there's no shame in that. No one, no matter how brilliant they are at what they do, can bat a thousand every time."

"And no one," he said slowly, icily, "no matter how good a job they think they're doing of keeping their business matters private can know when someone is snooping around in their business, can they?"

"You may characterize it as snooping, Rio, but it's really nothing more than good business sense on our part. Surely you didn't expect us to offer you as much money as we have without first finding out as much as possible about you."

He could feel himself starting to tremble with outrage. He couldn't remember ever being as angry as he was at that moment. He sprang up, and bracing his hands on the arms of her chair, he leaned over her until his face was inches from hers. "If you've never understood a word I've said to you before, then understand this." He spoke quietly from between clenched teeth. "I didn't ask for your offer. I didn't want it. I refused it in no uncertain terms, and I did so more than once. And I never, *ever*, once gave you reason to think I would change my mind. You had no right, Yasmine, to pry into my business." He straightened and pounded his fist against the wall. "*No . . . damn . . . right.*"

Shaken to see him so upset, she held up a hand to him, hoping to make him see what had happened the way she did. "Rio, this is business. Anyone who gives you a contract will investigate you. Anyone who gives you any kind of credit will do the same thing. Even though you own your company lock, stock, and barrel, there's always information to be had."

"Not information like *you've* come up with, honey." His jaw clenched and unclenched. "Where did you get it?"

"You're missing the point," she said carefully.

"I got the point all right, sweetheart. You have an excellent aim, almost fatal, in fact." He was whispering. His anger was building into rage. "All I want to know is *how* and *where* you got your information."

She eyed him warily. "Wyatt picked up a very faint rumor, but he couldn't verify it."

"And this faint rumor . . . it was that I *might* be having financial difficulties?"

She nodded. "And that you were trying to get a loan."

"I see." Barely able to breathe, he moved away from her. He felt betrayed in some deep, elemental way by her. Irrational? Maybe, but that's the way he felt. But he also knew he had to gain control over his feelings. Yasmine would have to be blind not to see that he was angry, but he didn't want her to know how deeply his anger ran. Knowledge gave power, and as far as he was concerned, she already had too damn much knowledge.

He spun around and returned to his chair. She reached out a hand toward him as if she would touch him, but at the last moment she withdrew it. He was glad. In the mood he was in, he couldn't have said what he would have done to her if she'd touched him. Kill her, kiss her—at this moment to him it seemed all the same thing.

"I'm sure there's no information leak in your company, Rio, if that's what you're worried about. Your employees are all totally dedicated to you."

She sat primly with her hands folded in her lap, looking for all the world as innocent as a lamb, yet knowingly or unknowingly she'd already taken the first steps to bringing his world toppling down around him. "So after you and your cousin heard this faint rumor, what did you do?"

"What difference does it make, Rio? It still doesn't answer my question. Why won't you take the offer?"

"Humor me," he said with deadly softness.

She shifted uneasily in her seat, but she didn't drop her gaze from his nor try to evade his question. "As I said, Wyatt couldn't verify the rumor, but Saturday night, when I walked up on you and Penny, I saw her point out a man to you and tell you to go talk to him. I was curious, so the next day I described the man to Brent. Between Brent and Rachel, I found out the man was Tex Camden, a banker." She shrugged. "It gave Wyatt another avenue to investigate."

"How proud your family must be of you," he drawled sarcastically. "No one can say you don't have brains beneath all that beauty." He surged up from his chair, grabbed a tennis ball, and began hurling it at the wall. The bulletin board shook every time the ball slammed against the wall, but it was either that or strangle her. Unfortunately he hadn't completely ruled out the latter. The ball came screaming back at him. He tore it from the air and wheeled on her. "Who else knows? Who did your cousin talk to?"

"Only a couple of people who Wyatt trusts."

"*No one* can be trusted when it comes to money, don't you know that, honey? Hell, as soon as your cousin hung up his phone, those two people talked to two other people, who talked to two other people, and so on and so on."

"*Stop* calling me honey and sweetheart in that denigrating tone," she said quietly. "And it doesn't matter who talks to whom. No one will outbid DI."

Despite his best intentions, he exploded. "You just don't friggin' *get* it, do you?" His arms shot out and his hands closed tightly around her shoulders and he hauled her to her feet. "The first time you came here, I asked you if you would lose anything financially or emotionally if I didn't take your offer. Your answer was that it was very important to DI to acquire my company. What I didn't tell you then, but what I will tell you now is that my company is my *blood*. My *lifeblood*. Do you get it now? This is my *life* you're playing with."

"I'm not playing," she said as calmly as before, but her skin had paled. "Anyone else would be ecstatic with the amount of money I've offered you, Rio."

He felt as if he might throw up. It was as if they weren't talking the same language. His hands tightened on her arms and he lightly shook her. "What in the hell do I have to do to make you understand I'm *not* anyone?"

"I do understand that, Rio," she said, her tone infuriatingly reasonable. "You're an incredibly talented man, which is why we want your company and why we want you."

"Damn you, Yasmine," he said, his teeth bared, his voice a harsh growl. "You've got an answer for everything, but you don't *listen* to me when I say something. You don't *believe* me when I say my company is not for sale." He jerked a thumb to one of the photographs behind him. "You see that old wildcatter up there on the wall. When he'd go bust, he'd pack it up and move on. It was hard as hell on his wife and child, but I don't have a wife and child. Before I'd work for the Damarons, I'd do the exact same thing."

"And lose everything you've worked for?" Her brow wrinkled deeply. "Throw your friends out of work? Destroy something fine? I don't understand that."

He released her with a slight push and deliberately moved away from her. "No, you don't, because up until now I'm sure no one has ever said no to you and meant it. You walk into a company with all your money and they just roll over, don't they? And if it doesn't happen the first time, then you open up their business for inspection, snoop into their financial records, undermine them with rumor and innuendo, hang their guts out to dry, and then come at them again."

The need to do something violent was building in him. He was so angry, he was about to choke with it. The one thing, the *only* thing that was keeping him from exploding was the knowledge that all the violence and shouting in the world wasn't going to do him a bit of good. He *had* to get his anger under control so that he could think. He *had* to decide what to do next in order to control the damage already done to his company by the rumor. It was imperative that no more damage be done. He needed spin control, time . . .

"Rio, I'm not going to apologize for doing my job. But I am sorry if you feel something I've done has inadvertently hurt you or your company."

He turned slowly toward her. Standing where he'd left her, she was chalk white and swaying slightly. She'd faced his anger, was *still* facing his anger, and hadn't once backed down from him. Beauty *and* guts were a lethal combination. He didn't know what he was going to do about her, but he knew he had to do something. "That's very kind of you," he said, each word a sharp jab in spite of his effort to keep his voice even.

She made a graceful gesture with her hand. "I know you're angry now, Rio, but you and I are seeing this *so* differently that I still don't entirely understand why."

"You mean other than the fact that you and your cousin stuck your noses into something that was none of your business and then had the audacity to call it good business practice? Or do you mean other than the fact that you apparently can't take no for an answer no matter how many times I say it?"

"When you cool down," she said, ignoring his outburst, "I think you'll see that no real harm has been done. As I said before, Wyatt spoke only to people he trusted."

He folded his arms across his chest and walked to her. "Then help me."

"Help you what?"

"Help me cool down." Without really knowing what he was doing, he reached out for her and drew her to him.

Her eyes widened in surprise. "How?"

"By changing the subject," he said gruffly, gratified to finally hear uncertainty in her voice. Apparently he'd at last succeeded in shaking her up, but whatever uncertainty he had managed to rouse in her, it wasn't enough to satisfy him. "And by making love with me."

Before she could say anything, he brought his lips down hard on hers, the force of his kiss opening her mouth. Then his tongue stroked in deeply, demanding, taking, and his hands slid over her back and down to her bottom, where his strong, lean fingers cupped her and arched her against his rigid sex.

Yasmine's heart lurched and her legs went weak. Once again she realized Rio was trying to use her. But instead of using her as a diversion as he had tried on Saturday night, he was now trying to use her to soothe the anger still boiling inside him. Then again, maybe he was simply trying to make her pay in some way. Whatever his reasons, it didn't seem to matter to her, at least not at the moment. The heat she was feeling was like nothing before. Her lower body throbbed with it. Her veins were filled with it. Her throat ached with it. And she was in serious danger of coming apart inside.

He backed her against the door, his mouth taking hers time after time, then he began tugging her skirt upward. She intended to make a sound of protest, but it turned into a sound of pleasure.

"Why in hell did you have to come into my life?" he muttered harshly, his lips pressed against hers. "And why in hell do I have to want you so damn much?"

The questions were rhetorical, which was good, she thought, because she didn't have any answers. In fact, she was asking herself the exact same questions, in particular the latter. Why did she have to want him so damn much?

She hadn't known how much she wanted him until he'd pulled her against him. She hadn't known how much she'd missed his lips against hers until he'd started kissing her once more.

She could no longer hear sounds coming from the other room. Only the pounding of her heart filled her ears. Then with an ease that took her breath away, he stroked his fingers beneath her panties to the moist, silky depths of her, and she could no longer hear her heartbeat. She clutched at his broad shoulders and gasped as he gently caressed and rubbed. And then she came undone.

Someone knocked on the door right behind her, and he jerked.

"Rio?" Penny called.

He groaned as he raised his head. "I'll be out in a minute," he said, his voice hoarse and thick.

"Is everything all right?" Penny asked after a moment's hesitation.

"Fine." He looked down at Yasmine, his dark eyes glittering fiercely. "Give me a few minutes."

"Okay," Penny called back.

Yasmine gazed up at Rio, her heart still pounding like a wild thing. His kisses had left her lips swollen, his touches had left her aching.

He dipped his head and pressed his lips against hers one last time, then lifted his body away from hers and straightened, leaving her feeling empty and lost and wanting to cry.

With shaking hands she tried to bring some order to her clothes, but she soon realized she was making no headway. Rio pushed her hands away. Quickly, efficiently, he pulled her skirt down and straightened her blouse and jacket.

"That will have to do for now," he murmured.

She tried to smooth her hair into place, but he took over that task too, even retying the satin ribbon into its usual bow.

His gray eyes were dark and moody as he spread his long fingers along either side of her face. "I'll make you a deal, Yasmine."

She wasn't certain what she expected after what had just happened between them, but it hadn't been that he would propose a deal. "What kind of a deal?"

"I'll take a few days and give serious consideration to your offer *if* you'll give serious consideration to making love with me."

She couldn't have said which part of his deal stunned her more. Finally, for the first time, he was saying that he would actually *consider* her offer—but only *if* . . . She stared up at him, dumbfounded.

"I'm perfectly serious," he said huskily. "Tell your cousin to stop making inquiries into my company so that I can have some breathing room, and I promise I'll give a great deal of thought to your offer." He paused and caressed her face. "And as for you making love with me . . ." He shrugged. "Well, why not?" he asked softly. "That way we'll both have a chance at getting something we each want."

Perhaps the correct response would have been to tell him to go straight to hell, but she didn't have it in her. The deal only called for her to contemplate the possibility of making love with him. Hell, she did that every time he smiled at her or reached out and touched her. "All right," she whispered.

Rio sank into his chair and rubbed his face wearily. Every muscle in his body hurt, he was tired, and he didn't know if he'd ever be able to get up again. He felt as if he'd fought a battle.

God, but he'd been a bastard to Yasmine, but he hadn't been able to help himself. Everything he'd said or done had been instinctive. He'd been fighting to protect his company and himself.

When he'd found out Yasmine knew about his money problems, he'd gone ballistic. He'd wanted to hit out at the person who, it had seemed at the time, had just driven the final nail into his coffin.

He rested his head against the back of his chair. He'd wanted to strangle her, then, amazingly, hunger and need had rushed up inside him, pushing aside the anger. He hadn't been able to see or think of anything but her and how she smelled, tasted, felt. And she'd wanted him too. If he didn't know anything else about her, he knew that.

Then Penny had knocked on the door, breaking through the haze of desire that had gripped him, and he'd looked down at Yasmine and suddenly he'd known he was going to have to lie to her. It had been all about giving himself time.

Truthfully he wouldn't, couldn't consider her offer. Selling his company would be selling himself. And no matter what DI promised, they'd have too much money invested in him to risk giving him the autonomy he needed and craved. They would tie him into knots with their policies and procedures. There'd always be someone looking over his shoulder. No, he couldn't sell.

But if saying he'd think about the offer would keep her and her cousin quiet about his problems even a few more days, it would be well worth the lie.

Rumors, good and bad, spread fast and could destroy a reputation in the blink of an eye. If his reputation went, everything else would go too. Even the possibility of a loan would disappear, and after that, the contract could be pulled. Certainly there'd be no confidence in Tsunami even if he was able to get it out. He'd lose everything he'd worked so hard to achieve.

So he'd told a lie and gambled that she'd buy it. He'd been pretty sure she would, since it was the first time he'd indicated he would even consider the offer. He was also gambling that with the extra days, he'd be able to complete Borggeo-Wagner.

And he hadn't promised Yasmine he'd *take* the deal, only that he'd *think* about it. And likewise, he hadn't asked her to make love with him, only to *think* about it.

She wouldn't, of course. As much as he wanted her, and as much as she might want him, she wouldn't consent to make love with him. He saw her as a danger to him, because she had the power to ruin his company. But for some reason he hadn't yet figured out, she was also wary of him. Perhaps because of their obvious intense attraction for each other. Toss two lighted sticks of dynamite together and you got a huge explosion.

If she came around during the next few days or contacted him, trying to feel him out about his thoughts on the offer, he planned to string her along until it was safe for him to give her a definite no again. Then she'd be out of his life for good.

As for his business, he could see only one course of action. He had to break through the wall of the Borggeo-Wagner application, get it done as quickly as possible, and get the final payment for it. Then he had to work out the final bugs on Tsunami, put the finishing touches on it, and get it out on the market. And there was no room for failure in any of those steps.

SIX

Rachel came to a surprised halt just inside the doorway of her large country kitchen. "You went to the grocery store, Yasmine?"

"Yes." Yasmine deposited several grocery sacks on the oak island in the center of the kitchen.

"But why? With all the food and drinks we bought for the party, I thought we had everything anyone could possibly want here."

"You do." Yasmine glanced at Rachel, wondering what her reaction was going to be when she heard the real reason behind the shopping trip. "I just didn't know what I wanted, so I decided to go to the grocery store and look around."

"Oh, hey—you want to talk about food cravings? Then I'm your girl. You wouldn't believe some of the foods I've been craving lately." Rachel cheerfully made her way over to the island and plopped her knitting bag down. "So? What'd you get?" With a hand supporting her back, she peered into one of the grocery sacks. "Long-neck beer and champagne? Honey, we've got a huge stash of both of these here."

"Yeah, I know, but there were other things I thought I needed."

Rachel pulled out a basket of strawberries, a can of whipped cream, and a brick of cream cheese, and held them up inquiringly.

Yasmine shrugged. "I couldn't decide. What do you think? Whipped cream and strawberries, or cream cheese and strawberries?"

"Why not both? Oh, hey, listen, here's an idea for you. The other night I put strawberries in an onion sandwich, and you can't *believe* the fabulous taste."

"You're right. I can't. What's more, I don't want to." Yasmine turned to the next sack and pulled out a big bucket of spicy chicken wings.

With a chuckle, Rachel rooted through another sack. "Okay, we've got caviar—a very good brand, I might add." She suddenly glanced at her friend. "*Caviar?* Uh-oh. You've got a classic case of menu indecision going on here, honey. Long-neck beer and spicy chicken wings *or* champagne, strawberries, and caviar, but I wouldn't think both."

Yasmine quietly sighed. "Yeah, I know."

"And . . . *What in the world?*" Rachel's eyes widened as she pulled out a small box of condoms from the last bag. "Yasmine Damaron, I can*not* believe what I am seeing."

"Give me that." She stretched across the island and grabbed the box out of Rachel's hand.

"Whoa, whoa, *whoa*. Yasmine? Have you been keeping something from me?"

Yasmine's lips twisted ruefully. "Obviously not. Do you have a big wicker basket around here somewhere? Or maybe two medium-size ones?"

"In the cupboard behind you. So *give*. What's the deal with the *condoms*? What could have possibly happened since I saw you at breakfast?"

"It's complicated."

"A man, huh?"

"You know me—I believe in being prepared."

With a perplexed expression on her face, Rachel moved away to the breakfast nook, carrying her knitting bag with her. "Okay," she said, settling herself at the maple table, "I can see you're going to be no help, but it's all right. Don't tell me anything. I can work my way through this on my own. It won't even be much of a challenge. So let's see . . ." She tapped her fingernails on the tabletop. "Well, you say you believe in being prepared— by the way, tell me something I *don't* know—and so you went out and bought a package of condoms." She thought for a moment and then grinned. "So far I'm doing well, don't you think?"

Yasmine folded the grocery sacks and put them away. "So far you haven't told me anything I haven't already told you."

Rachel frowned at her. "Hang on, hang on, I'm just getting warmed up. So, okay, obviously nothing is definite yet, but you're thinking sex is a possibility." She looked at Yasmine, who stared impassively back at her, then Rachel suddenly brightened. "Actually, now that I'm really thinking, you probably think sex is much more than a possibility. My heavens"—she slapped her forehead— "with *Rio* in the picture, who *wouldn't* be thinking that?" Yasmine's impassivity broke and Rachel clapped her hands together in glee. "Ha! I knew it—I'm *right*. Am I good or am I good?" She hit the table with the flat of her hand. "Man, I'm *good*."

Yasmine's eyes narrowed. "If you can stop congratulating yourself long enough, I'd like a little advice."

"Honey, sweetie, sugar pie! The last time you took my advice on anything was in the seventh grade, when you asked me what I thought about Gerald McHenry and I told you I thought he was a geek."

Yasmine sank into a chair across from Rachel. "Yeah, and by the time we were seniors he was the football captain, president of the senior class, and had been chosen Most Likely to Succeed."

Rachel shook her head. "He wasn't right for you, trust me."

"Well, I never had the chance to find out, did I? Once I gave him the brushoff, Julie Bennett got her claws into him and never let go."

Rachel threw up her hands. "A perfect example of the saying, there's no accounting for taste."

"Oh, who cares." Yasmine abruptly sat forward.

"This is the deal, Rach. Remember yesterday when I told you Rio had finally agreed to think about my offer?"

"Uh-huh."

"Well, he sort of made me a deal. He said he'd consider my offer if I would consider making love with him."

Rachel's mouth dropped open. "*Get out of town.*"

"That was the deal."

"*Wow.* Now, that's what I call an interesting deal." Her expression slowly turned serious. "So *that's* what your shopping spree was all about?"

"I plan to take him a picnic basket tonight."

"The forecast is calling for rain."

"I'm sure we'll be inside."

"*Wow.*"

"Could you please get beyond the wow and give me some advice?"

"Right away, and here it is. A deal that requires the two parties to only *think* about something is not much of a deal."

Yasmine groaned. "Don't you think I know that? But, Rach, since I saw Rio yesterday at his office, I haven't been able to think about anything else *but* making love with him." She paused. "Truthfully, even before that."

Rachel waved at the grocery items stacked on the kitchen island behind her. "Well, it looks to me as if you've made up your mind."

She nodded. "I have."

"Okay, so then *why* don't you look happier?"

She sighed. "You know how you told me that one day I'd learn there are some things in life that I simply can't control?"

Rachel nodded. "Sure."

"Well, I've learned. This attraction I feel for Rio is way beyond my control, though it's taken me this long to admit it. But to make it worse, I know it's not the same for him."

"I don't believe that. He wouldn't have come up with the deal if he didn't—"

"Oh, he wants me, all right. I don't have a doubt in my mind about that. I also don't have a doubt in my mind that I'm nothing more than a diversion for him, just like one of his surfing trips."

"Honey, no man in his right mind would think of you as nothing more than a surfing trip."

Yasmine chuckled humorlessly. "You and I have already had this talk, remember? Since then I've decided that I overreacted when Rio asked me to leave your party and go home with him, because I knew then what was going on. It was and is very clear that he wants only a fling, and I guess the fact in some way hurt my feelings."

"But you don't know how?"

"Not really. Except no man has ever asked me to have a fling with him unless he was drunk and/or wanted money. I know for a fact Rio was not drunk and he absolutely, positively doesn't want my money. No." She shook her head. "His motives are pure. He simply wants to have sex with me for no other reason than to have sex."

"I see," Rachel said slowly. "And everything you just said means *what*?"

"That my feelings were hurt."

Rachel dropped her head in her hand. "My baby must have sucked out all my brain cells, because I'm not getting what your problem is."

"Never mind. I probably don't either. But I *have* thought a lot about my reaction and what would have happened if I'd gone with him."

Rachel propped her elbow on the table and rested her chin on her hand. "I bet it wouldn't have been unbearable, that's for sure." Her voice was soft and faraway and Yasmine realized that Rachel's mind had wandered to that imagined night with Rio.

Yasmine snapped her fingers in front of Rachel's face to regain her attention. "Anyway, I've made a decision. I'm a big girl, I can take care of myself, I've got my eyes wide open, I want to make love with him, and I'm going to be fine."

Rachel gazed at her anxiously. "I hope so, honey, but I've got to point out that you've never done anything like this before. I mean, you've had *one* very carefully thought out, very carefully prepared for affair your entire life, and that was in college with a guy you dated for *eleven months* before you let him progress beyond a kiss and come home with you."

Yasmine shook her head. "I can't see Rio waiting eleven months for any woman."

"Forget Rio. I'm talking about *you* now. What is it you want?"

Yasmine smiled. "Rio."

Rachel's anxious expression didn't change, and Yasmine exhaled a long breath. Worrying Rachel was the last thing she wanted to do, particularly now because of her pregnancy. "By the way," she said, inserting a deliberately casual tone into the conversation, "what's with the pink blanket?" She nodded toward the pink yarn spilling out of Rachel's knitting bag.

The change of subject did the trick. Rachel beamed.

"Today I'm almost positive I'm having a girl."

Yasmine laughed. "What happened to your little linebacker?"

"I decided the movements were more like pas de chat." Rubbing her stomach, Rachel nodded her head with a serene contentment. "Yes, I'm definitely having a girl."

"I'll order a pair of baby ballet shoes right away," Yasmine said dryly.

Yasmine pulled her car into the drive and turned off the ignition. Rain misted the windows as she gazed through the night at Rio's home on the rise above her. From her pre-meeting investigation of Rio, she knew the approximate value of his residence and that it sat in the middle of twenty acres, but the statistics she'd read couldn't begin to do justice to the charm of the relatively modest two-story log dwelling.

A stone chimney anchored one end of the house, a screened-in porch the other end, and in the center, log steps led up to the front porch and door. The rugged, rustic abode was nothing fancy, but it made perfect sense to her that Rio would have a home like this.

She climbed out of the car and reached for one of the two baskets she'd brought. Her nerves were strung tight, her skin felt flushed. After she'd gone only a short way, her heart was beating painfully hard.

She'd always been circumspect and deliberate in her dealings with men, both professionally and personally, but not with Rio. By coming to him, she'd well and truly thrown caution to the wind. She didn't know what would happen. She had no idea what the outcome would be. She knew only that there was no one else in the world she wanted to be with tonight except Rio.

The journey from the car to Rio's front door took everything she had, but once she was on the porch she felt a sense of elation, because in her own way, she was taking matters into her own hands.

True, she didn't have control over the erotic and turbulent emotions Rio stirred in her, or over the fact that he could make her want him more than any man ever had. But she'd given tonight a lot of thought and had tried to prepare herself. Rio wasn't the love of her life any more than her boyfriend in college had been. Rio was a complication she hadn't expected, a force she had to deal with. And if she didn't feel one hundred percent confident in herself and what she was about to do, she was at least satisfied that she knew *what* she was doing.

She was going to ask Rio to make love with her, because if she didn't, she would regret it for the rest of her life.

She knocked, and after a minute the door opened and Rio appeared. Warm, low-level light from the room beyond spilled out, backlighting his tall, lanky body. Wearing a wrinkled T-shirt and faded jeans, along with a slightly preoccupied expression, he looked as if he'd just climbed out of bed to answer the door, leaving a woman waiting for him, naked and sweaty. Mussed hair and bare feet enhanced the sensual intimacy of his look.

"Yasmine?"

"Hello, Rio."

His gaze swept over her, searched the area behind her, then came back to her. "What are you doing here?"

"It's nice to see you again too, Rio," she said evenly. "Aren't you going to invite me in?"

He moved aside, all his attention now focused on her. "By all means—come in."

Yasmine stepped into a large living room with exposed beams and a ceiling that soared two stories high. Comfortable-looking couches and chairs were arranged around a stone fireplace. Several fans turned slowly above them, and the plaintive sound of Billie Holiday drifted in the air. Across the room, a computer sat on a long table, its large-screened monitor on.

"You've been working?"

"Yes."

As usual, he wasn't helping her out by returning her social chatter, she thought, feeling both amusement and the slightest panic. "I like your home."

"I do too." Rio couldn't take his eyes off Yasmine. In fact, he could barely believe that she was there.

Her hair lay loose and gleaming around her shoulders, the silver streak shimmering through the topaz, its length spilling down the back of the cream-colored silk blouse she wore. The matching skirt stopped above her knee. Peach-colored toenails peeked out from open-toed cream leather sandals. She looked expensive and fragile, untouchable and desirable.

She seemed to grow more and more lovely each time he saw her, and he didn't understand how that could be, just as he didn't understand how his need for her kept building and building.

She smiled at him. "I've always liked hardwood floors."

He pushed the door shut and moved toward her. "What are you doing here, Yasmine?"

"At the moment I'm trying to make small talk."

Her eyes glittered with self-deprecating humor. "Quite unsuccessfully, I might add."

"I was working."

"So you said." She glanced at his computer, and he noted light threading through her hair, catching in the delicate streak of silver. "But I'm hoping you can take a break to eat." She gestured with the basket she was carrying. "Since I wasn't certain what you liked to eat, I brought a little of everything."

Her unexpected presence had caught him off guard, and he was at a loss for words. He hadn't even known she'd been in his mind until she had appeared, and then he'd realized she'd been there all along. A light mist of rain had dewed her face, her throat, and the skin left bare by the V of her neckline. It had also moistened her blouse, making it cling to her curves in a mind-flaming way.

Amid a night when there'd been only solitude and work, Yasmine's golden beauty, glimmering eyes, and perfumed scent were like a kick in the gut.

"Rio?"

"How did you even know I was here?" he asked huskily.

"I called your work and spoke to someone there."

A new CD whirled smoothly into place and then soft, improvisational jazz filled the room. "You're listening to jazz?"

"Yeah? So?"

"Nothing really, except you listen to rock at work."

"Every now and then I like a change."

A tentative smile touched her lips. "Then you're going to love this little picnic I brought, or at least I hope you are."

She turned and made her way across the large room to a corner and a round oak table and chairs. She deposited the basket on one of the chairs, drew out a tablecloth, flicked it open, and then let it settle over one end of the table. "Something told me you wouldn't have a tablecloth," she said lightly.

She was talking tablecloths and fussing around his table, while knots of wanting racked his insides, he reflected grimly. He barely resisted the urge to grab her to him and demand answers from her, but touching her would be a really bad idea. Right now he felt so off balance, he might not be able to control what he would do if he touched her. And no matter what had happened between them at his office yesterday, he still remembered her rejection of him Saturday night.

"What in hell are you doing, Yasmine?" he asked quietly.

"I've brought you dinner, but I'm pretty sure I've already said that." She drew two cream-colored wax candles from the basket. "I'm glad I put these in at the last minute, since I think candles and rainy nights go together, don't you?"

Her long legs stretched as she placed the candles in the center of the tablecloth, and after she'd lit their wicks, the flames flickered to life and the candle glow lovingly slid into the V between her breasts. "There," she said with satisfaction, standing back to admire her work.

Frustration mounted in him. Without even realizing what he was doing, he curled his fingers into his palms and clenched his teeth. Then he saw that her hands were shaking, and strangely, he felt a little better, knowing she wasn't as composed as she seemed. "Okay, Yasmine, skip right over the part about you bringing dinner, and candles, and tablecloths and get straight to the damn point. Did you come to talk about your offer? Is that what this is all about?"

She threw a glance up at him from the corner of her eye. "Sort of." She pulled a container of chicken wings out of the basket. "I was told these are very spicy, and since you're a Texan, I decided you probably liked spicy foods. If not, I have other things out in the car, but the potato salad and baked beans are to go with the chicken wings. *Do* you like spicy foods? Oh, and I've got a six-pack of beer out in the car and a bottle of champagne, whichever you prefer."

His expression darkened. "What do you mean *sort of*?"

"Let's eat first," she said with an attempt at brightness, busy bringing out more containers. "And by the way, if you don't want the chicken wings, I brought pâté de foie gras, smoked salmon, and strawberries, but they're in another basket out in the car." She straightened away from the table. "I'll just go get them."

His hand shot out and caught her arm before she could move. "*What* do you mean, sort of?" he asked quietly. "We made a deal yesterday, remember?"

She swallowed. "I remember."

"And it better damn well still be in effect."

His hand tightened on her arm. "Do *not* tell me your cousin has gone ahead with his little investigation of me. I'm living up to my part of our deal. I've been thinking about your offer."

Surprisingly the lie didn't come easily, and he realized that lying was something he'd never much bothered with before, especially to women. He'd always gone his own way and lived life on his terms, and if someone didn't like it, they were out of his life. But it wasn't the actual lying that was leaving a bad taste in his mouth, he realized. It was lying to *Yasmine*.

She pulled her arm from his grip. "This is not about your part of our deal."

The lines of his mouth hardened. "So what is it? Is your cousin putting the pressure on you to get an answer from me?"

"No. I spoke with him and told him it would be a few more days. He's fine with that."

"He's stopped his snooping?"

"He's stopped his business inquiries for now." She reached back into the basket.

"Then I'll ask you again. What in hell is this all about?"

"It's about *my* part of the bargain, Rio."

"Your part?"

She held out a condom to him. "You told me to think about making love with you, and I have. My answer is yes."

He stared at her, stunned. Never in a million years had he expected this. He'd made the last part of the deal for two reasons. One, because of the heat of the moment. He'd wanted her so badly that if Penny hadn't knocked on the door, he might have taken her right there in the office. Penny's interruption had been just what he'd needed to bring him back to reality.

The second reason was that he was deceiving her with *his* part of the bargain, and it had made him feel better to know she would *never* consider her part. Despite their obvious attraction for each other, he'd always known she was as wary of him as he was of her.

"You must know," he said, gritting the words out, "that I didn't actually expect you to seriously consider what I'd said."

"Why not?" she asked, her voice even, though her hands were still shaking. "Does that mean I shouldn't expect you to be seriously considering my offer?"

Rubbing the back of his neck, he let out a stream of curses. "No, that's not what I mean."

"Then does it mean that you've changed your mind and no longer want me?"

He sucked in his breath sharply. God help him, he wanted her more than ever. He whirled away from her, knowing it was folly to continue standing so close, but then he immediately turned back, unable to endure being too far away from her.

Anger and passion churned in him. He wanted to lash out and hurt her before he gave in to his feelings and made love to her and then ended up getting hurt himself. He paused in his thoughts. Funny. He had no idea where he had come up with the notion that he might get hurt. He immediately forgot about it.

"You know, I've always heard you Damarons were ruthless. People say you always get what you go after. My mistake was in not realizing just how far you'd go."

"What do you mean?"

"I mean you're willing to sacrifice your beautiful body on the altar of my bed for Damaron International so that I'll sell you my company."

She flinched as if he'd slapped her and the color drained from her face. "There's no reason to be cruel," she said quietly. "All you had to do was tell me that the last part of the deal was a joke and that you don't really want me, and I wouldn't have bothered you anymore." She stepped around him. "I'll be on my way."

She was halfway to the front door before he caught up with her. His hands closed around her wrist, drawing her to a stop. "I'm sorry. Okay? I'm sorry. But you walked into my house tonight, held out a condom to me, and told me you wanted to make love with me. How am I supposed to stay rational when you do something like that?"

"I don't think that's my problem," she said, a tremor running through her voice. "Good night."

"Wait." He drew in an uneven breath. "Yasmine . . ."

"You don't have to say anything else. I'm very sorry I disturbed you."

"Disturbed me?" He laughed mirthlessly, then took her face between his hands and gazed deeply into her eyes. "Yasmine, I can't even begin to tell you how much I want you, but I don't want you to feel that making love with me is some kind of obligation on your part because of what I said yesterday."

Her eyes clouded and her breasts rose and fell with her agitated breathing. "How stupid do you think I am, Rio? Do you honestly believe that's what I would think?"

He shook his head. "I didn't . . . I don't . . . ah, hell, Yasmine. When you and I get together, any semblance of rationality flies out the door."

She jerked away from him and a pulse beat madly at the base of her throat. "Then I'll leave and the problem will be solved."

"Don't go."

She stopped in her tracks. Slowly she turned to him. "Why not?"

His throat suddenly felt painfully tight. He wasn't even sure he'd be able to speak. "Because . . . I very badly want you to stay."

Her gaze was defiant. "Why?"

"Because I want to make love with you more than I can say. But . . ."

She folded her arms beneath her breasts. "But what, Rio? Are you about to make me another deal? You know, you may have actually missed your calling. You're better at deal making than I am."

"Yasmine . . ." He shook his head. "I just want you to be absolutely sure that staying is what you want."

"I believe I've already indicated that."

Rio looked at Yasmine. Even in the dim light of the room, she had an exquisite golden glow about her. Every muscle in his body was hard and his blood was pounding through his veins. He was right smack in the middle of the worst crisis of his life, and she was very much a part of that crisis. Yet he wanted her with a passion that shook him to his very core. He went to her and framed her face with his trembling hands. "This is crazy—you know that, don't you?"

"I know," she said, gazing up at him.

"Are you sure?" he asked one last time.

She couldn't have been more sure, Yasmine reflected, tingling with excitement and desire. She didn't know where the certainty came from. Right from the first, their relationship had been stormy and her emotions had been confused and conflicted. So far, tonight had been no exception. She fully expected what was about to happen to raise even more questions and problems between them, but she couldn't think beyond tonight. Despite her shopping trip that morning and the hours of thought she'd given to this moment, she felt she was being impetuous for the first time in her life, and it was wonderful.

As an answer to his question, she thrust her fingers up into his hair and pulled his head down until his mouth touched hers.

With a groan he wrapped his arms around her and deepened the kiss. One hand slid down to her bottom to cup and hold her to his hard erection. The other hand spread across her back in a strong band that crushed her breasts against his chest. His tongue made forceful, intimate invasions into her mouth. It was as if a dam had broken inside him and released a flood of passion and she was the willing, greedy recipient of it all.

And then suddenly, kissing was no longer enough. She began to pull away from him just as he impatiently tore his mouth from hers.

"Come with me," he said, his breathing raspy, his eyes dark.

At that moment she would have followed him anywhere, but she knew where she wanted to go. "To your bedroom?"

With a nod, he tugged her toward the stairs. "If we stay here a second longer, our first time will be on the floor."

Their first time. Her heart leapt into her throat. He was saying there would be a second time, she thought with a thrill. She'd brought a small box of condoms, but only in case the one they first tried to use broke.

In his bedroom he turned her to him and kissed her once again. Only this time he did it gently, seductively, as his deft fingers went to the buttons of her blouse.

She closed her eyes and soaked up the sensations. Somewhere stereo speakers played soft jazz that curled around her with a seductive rhythm, and from outside she could hear the sounds of the rain as it drummed against the windows, heavier now than when she'd arrived. Rio murmured to her and kissed her face and neck, and the blouse whispered off her shoulders, down her arms, and then floated away. Her skirt drifted away in much the same manner. A cooling air caressed her bare skin, along with Rio's strong hands. He reached behind her to unfasten her bra. It vanished. Then slowly, purposefully, he stroked and massaged her hips and the long length of her legs until her panties were gone and she was completely naked.

The sensuality of the moment nearly shattered her. Opening her eyes, she looked up at him and saw his features drawn tight and tense with passion, then she gasped as he bent to her nipple, nibbled, then sucked it into his mouth.

Pleasure liquefied her bones, heat pooled in her loins. With a soft cry she grasped a handful of his T-shirt and began pulling it off him, but he frustrated her efforts by picking her up and carrying her to the bed, where he laid her down on a spread, soft and cool to her skin.

Her body aching for him, she lay there and watched hungrily as he stripped until finally his body was as naked as hers. Just looking at him made her mouth go dry. His torso was strong, his belly flat, his legs muscled, and his male length was aroused, full, and throbbing.

She held up her arms and he came down to her.

"I want to learn everything there is to learn about your body," he murmured, then set out to explore her inch by inch.

She clutched at his shoulders. "But I don't think I can wait long. Ah . . ." Heat shot down to her loins, and her hips lifted and undulated. "What are you doing?"

"Waiting," he whispered as his hands discovered curving contours of her body and his tongue found secret crevices and creases.

"No," she said.

He didn't respond because his mouth was involved with another part of her body.

Caress by caress, touch by touch, she went slowly mad. She moaned and cried out and clawed, but he paid her no heed. Sensation topped sensation. Fires started other more intense fires. She went over one peak after another peak until she was certain she couldn't take any more.

Then he moved over her and with one long, powerful stroke, he thrust into her, filling her, claiming her, and she knew she'd only just begun.

SEVEN

Sometime in the night a violent spring storm broke over them. Lightning ripped through the darkness, flashing incandescent light into the bedroom. Thunder boomed over their heads, shaking the house.

Yasmine barely noticed. The storm of passion raging inside her was every bit as furious and powerful as the one raging around them. When Rio had begun to make love to her, the world as she knew it stopped . . . began again . . . then changed forever.

She'd lost her virginity years earlier, but she felt as if Rio were the first man she'd ever made love with. During the long hours of the night, Rio taught her unexpected things about sex, astounding, marvelous things, even shocking things, but she never once pulled back. Instead, she'd basked in their profound intimacy, came alive, begged for more.

There'd been no part of her body he hadn't touched and kissed. Her skin became so sensitive that when he lightly blew a warm breath over her breasts, she cried out with pleasure at the exquisite torment.

Once he left her to set a match to the stacked logs in the fireplace. Almost immediately a fire blazed up, sending its warmth out to dispel the chill in the room that she hadn't even been aware of until then. Actually, until then she hadn't even known there was a fireplace in the room. Later, she promised herself, she would explore his home, but then immediately forgot about the promise as he returned to her, climbing onto the bed. For a moment his naked body loomed over her, but then she reached for him, brought him down to her, and wrapped her arms and legs tightly around him.

"I could strangle on this need I feel for you," he whispered, then with a rough groan penetrated her again.

Shuddering with sensations, she arched up to him and took him deep inside her.

The scent of sex and desire permeated the air, as did their shouts and cries. The night went on, and they became so tangled up in each other, she didn't see how they'd ever be able to pull apart. They made love until they were both on the verge of collapse, and still they remained ready for more, each time their need for each other stronger than the last.

Yasmine wasn't certain what woke her. It could have been the thunder rumbling in the distance as the storm moved away. Or it could have been the rain pelting the roof. But more than likely, she reflected, it was the unfamiliar presence of Rio beside her and the weight of his arm across her stomach, pinning her to the bed.

She moved her head along the pillow to look at him. He was sleeping deeply, his chest rising and falling with easy, even breaths, his body completely relaxed. She should be asleep too. She was physically exhausted, but, strangely, she also felt exhilarated.

She couldn't inhale without breathing in his musky male scent. She couldn't exhale without feeling the heat of his body against hers. And she couldn't think of anything else but their lovemaking. He'd been gentle, powerful, generous, demanding, and she'd never be the same again.

From this point forward she knew she'd use Rio as a yardstick to measure any man who ventured into her life, and she knew before it even happened that no matter who the man was, he would fall terribly short.

Rio rolled toward her and pulled her against his hard, naked body. She waited to see what he'd do next, then realized he'd reached out for her in his sleep. She felt a stirring near her heart.

This night with Rio would never come again, and she wanted to stay awake and experience and savor every moment. But soon Rio's warmth wrapped around her, his strength enfolded her, and despite her best intentions, she once again fell asleep.

When next Yasmine woke, gray light showed at the window and the rain had stopped. The night was drawing to an end, she sadly realized.

Carefully she eased from beneath Rio's arm and slipped from the bed. Never having been in the room before, it took her a moment to get her bearings. The bed, she saw, was wide and long and made out of oak with short, thick posts at each corner. A quilt lay in a heap on the floor. The fire had burnt down, but small flames still licked at the remaining wood. On the other side of the room a door stood open—the bathroom.

As quickly and quietly as she could, she washed herself. The warm, soapy washcloth was a balm to her sensitized skin, yet it did nothing to erase the pleasurable feel of Rio's touch. Warmth still ran along her nerves, her muscles still quivered with need, and she realized with amazement that she wanted him again.

When would she stop wanting him? she wondered. When a few hours had passed? When she went back home to New York and resumed her normal life? Or would it take weeks, months, years? Would she *ever* stop wanting him?

Right now it didn't seem as if she would, but she had to be wrong. Otherwise the coming days would be unbearable.

She squeezed a line of toothpaste onto her finger and brushed her teeth as best she could, but a few thrusts of her fingers through her hair did nothing to put it back in order. She gave up and was about to leave, when she caught a glimpse of herself in the mirror. After several moments' inspection, she realized there were no bruises on her skin. She was astonished. It wasn't that their lovemaking had been that rough, but it had been intense and hard, and she felt as if Rio had left some sort of indelible brand on her.

Back in the bedroom, she saw that he was still asleep. No wonder, she reflected with compassion. He'd looked tired ever since she'd known him. Perhaps he would at last get some rest.

She glanced around the room, but in the dim light she couldn't see any of her clothes. Then she practically stumbled over Rio's T-shirt.

She scooped it up, slipped it over her head, and immediately was engulfed by Rio's scent. For a split second she was tempted to go back to bed to cuddle next to him. But, no, he needed to sleep, so she made herself venture downstairs.

She'd received only a general impression of the main room when she'd arrived the previous night.

Her mind had been on Rio, and she hadn't noticed any of the details. Now, though, she gazed around her with interest.

As she might have expected, Rio didn't go in for a lot of knickknacks. There were a few framed photographs on a sofa table, one of his grandfather standing along the banks of a river, the Rio Grande, she guessed. Another picture showed his parents, standing in a yard beside what must have been a new car. The last photograph she saw stopped her in her tracks. It was another picture of Rio's grandfather, but this time he had a little boy of about nine beside him. *Rio.*

She picked up the picture and studied it more closely. An adorable little boy with bright, intelligent eyes and a great big grin of enthusiasm on his face stared back at her. She traced her fingertip along the line of the grin, one untouched by worry or weariness, and she couldn't help but wonder what Rio's face would look like today if he didn't shoulder the cares and concerns he now did. With all her heart she wished that the boy could give her clues to the man he had become, but then, no photograph could ever reveal the complexities of a man like Rio. She replaced the picture and continued her tour.

An afghan that might have been knitted by a mother or a grandmother was thrown over a chair. Books about computers were piled everywhere. On one short shelf was a mix of pleasure reading, a few were about Texas. A tall wrought-iron candle holder held a cream-colored candle that had never been lit. She could see no plants anywhere.

She walked over to the oak table and the basket she'd brought the night before. The chicken wings, along with many of the other things she'd brought, would have to be thrown out. As for the condoms, they hadn't used them. They'd used his, which had been upstairs in his bedside table drawer.

In this day and age it was a necessity for anyone who dated, man or woman, to have precautions on hand. It didn't necessarily mean that person was promiscuous—only wise and thoughtful of their partner. Intellectually she knew that. But emotionally all she could think of was that he'd made love with other women, and her heart hurt because of it.

How irrational.

A week ago she hadn't even met Rio. He'd had a life before her. He'd have a life after she left. She had no right to be jealous of other unknown women. But the fact remained that she was.

She glanced over at his computer. A pterodactyl was tormenting a Tyrannosaurus rex on the screen saver. Suddenly she realized that Rio hadn't had a chance to clear the screen after she'd arrived the previous night. Whatever he'd been working on would still be there, and she could retrieve it with a flick of her finger.

She was badly tempted.

It made sense that the reason Rio needed money was that he was having problems with something he was working on, which was causing delays. The Borggeo-Wagner contract? She'd be stunned if that was the case. She knew what the contract consisted of and she knew Rio's abilities. He was more than capable of fulfilling the contract.

She started toward the computer, but then stopped herself. *No.* Each time she'd walked into his office, Rio had cleared the screen, and his secrecy was understandable. Theirs was a highly competitive field, and he had not yet signed with Damaron International. Until he did, they were still competitors in the same marketplace. It would be unethical of her to look at his work without his permission.

The picture of the little boy and his grandfather drew her back. The nine-year-old Rio beamed at her. It was obvious he was feeling very big and very proud to be with his grandfather on their marvelous adventure. What a wonderful little boy he must have been.

And he'd grown into a brilliant, fiercely independent, moody, and complex man whom she'd come to town to buy and stayed to . . . She nearly dropped the picture.

She'd come to town to buy Rio and she'd stayed to fall in love with him. He might not have left a mark on her skin during their lovemaking, but he had left marks all over her heart, beginning the day she met him.

She was in love with him. God, why hadn't she realized what was happening sooner?

She had fallen in love with Rio Thornton.

"What's got you so fascinated?" Rio asked in a drowsy voice. On bare feet he padded across the floor and came up behind her.

Ridiculously, she felt frozen, unable to turn around. "Nothing . . . the picture . . ."

He slid an arm around her waist and pulled her back against him. His skin was warm even though a slight chill hung in the room. "What picture?" Reaching around her, he took the picture out of her hands. "That was a good trip," he said, and returned it to its place on the table.

Tears welled in her eyes. He'd casually dismissed the picture, but in the short time she'd held it in her hands and studied it, the little boy had come to mean so much to her. She was being a first-class idiot, she thought angrily, and quickly blinked the tears away.

She turned in his arms and gazed up at him in a new way, a way that was entirely about loving him. She wasn't afraid that he would see the love. Love would be the last thing on his mind. His work would be first, of course. What else? she wondered. She'd give a lot to know.

He'd pulled on a pair of jeans. His torso was bare, his hair tousled, his eyes still slumberous, his jaw darkened by a day and a night's growth of beard. "You looked so happy in that picture," she said.

"I was happy." He lifted both hands to push the cloud of hair back from her face. "I always had a great time whenever I was with my grandfather."

"He must have been very proud of you."

"In his eyes I could do no wrong, even when I did."

She smiled up at him, pleased to have this quiet moment with him before she had to get dressed and leave. "All children need unconditional love."

"Uh-huh." He rubbed his fingers up the side of her neck and back down again. "I'm not at all sad right now, you know," he said softly. "For one thing, seeing you in my T-shirt makes me *very* happy. For another . . ." He ran his hand beneath the shirt to her warm skin. "I'm absolutely *crazy* about the fact that you don't have anything on underneath it."

The laugh she'd intended to make turned into a gasp when his long fingers stroked down between her thighs. His touch was pure possessiveness as if the night they'd just spent together had given him the right to touch her in any way he wanted. She would have thought her newly discovered love for him might have made her shy, but her desire for him was powerful and strong and she welcomed his caresses. As a wave of heat swept over her, she moaned and dropped her head to his shoulders.

He pressed his mouth to her neck. "Are you hungry?"

Unable to answer, she simply shook her head. Emotions clogged her throat. Her body pulsed with a heavy, sweet fire. She was ready and aching for him once again.

"Are you sure you're not hungry?" he asked

thickly, smoothing his other hand up her abdomen and taking possession of one breast.

"The food I brought . . ."

"No longer good?" His finger brushed back and forth across her distended nipple while he continued to probe and caress the moist depths between her legs.

"Ah . . ." She climaxed, coming apart in his arms right there and then.

Her legs gave out from under her, and he scooped her up into his arms. She didn't know where he was carrying her, and she didn't care. She threaded her arms around his neck and held on as the fiery heat slowly ebbed from her body, leaving her weak.

Rio lowered her to a rug in front of the fireplace. The fire he'd started the night before had long since burned out. But he didn't need a fire to heat his body. He was hot and trembling with a need and hunger that he would never have thought possible. Surely wanting someone as much and as often as he wanted Yasmine had to be a kind of madness.

But if he was going to go mad, he wanted it to be while he was buried deep inside Yasmine. She was soft, silky, and golden, with hair that sometimes wrapped around him when he was holding her and a passion strong enough to match his.

"Why can't I get enough of you?" he asked, his voice low and rough. He shoved his jeans down around his knees and pushed her T-shirt above her

breasts. Without answering, she spread her thighs,
and with a harsh groan he thrust deeply into her
tight, moist flesh. She arched her hips, accepting
him even deeper, and he lost whatever semblance
of reason and vestige of control he'd managed to
hold on to until then.

He drove into her time after time, as hard as he
could, as fast as he could. She writhed and bucked
beneath him, wild, earthy, responsive, a dream crying out and raking her nails along his back. Ecstasy
beyond imagination suffused him. Twice she stiffened and cried out, twice her inner muscles con-
tracted around him, milking him, but he barely
gave heed. He didn't want to stop, nor could he
make himself stop.

He was caught up in a savage storm that was of
his own making. Lightning scored through him
each time he surged into her. Thunder resounded
and vibrated in him as her hips undulated and
arched beneath him.

Tension and wanting tightened in him, in-
creased, built, until it was beyond his endurance.
He closed his eyes and a deep hoarse sound erupted
from his chest as the powerful force of his passion
overcame him. Completely mindless, blind to everything but his own need, he exploded and emp-
tied himself into her.

Intense satisfaction mingled inside Rio, along
with puzzling fear. The satisfaction was easy to un-

derstand, the fear wasn't. He pushed the fear to the back of his mind, unwilling to think about it now.

His body curled around Yasmine from behind, spoon fashion. He pulled her closer against him and buried his face in her hair. At the same time, he ran his hand up and down her arm. Her skin was a never-ending source of wonder to him, soft as silk and lustrous as gold. She felt delicate and femininely fragile in his arms.

"You must be hungry now," he said.

"No." Her voice was so faint, he had to raise himself up on one elbow and bend his head to hear her.

Noting the paleness of her skin, he felt a surge of guilt. She had to be exhausted. After last night he should have been able to leave her alone. That he hadn't been able to just might be the cause of the puzzling fear he felt. Making love to her had been more of a compulsion than a need.

He was also feeling a large measure of self-disgust. Without realizing his deceit, she'd bought in to the deal he'd made her, and believing that he was living up to his part of it, she'd lived up to her part. When she'd showed up on his doorstep with food and condoms, he should have sent her home, but he hadn't been able to. He'd needed her, he'd wanted her, he'd taken her, and if he had it to do over again, he'd do the same thing.

Once again he pushed the thoughts to the back of his mind. Holding her against him, with her hips nestled against his pelvis, he could pretend that for this moment in time she was his. "Are you cold?"

"No."

"Thirsty?"

"Yes."

He smoothed the hair away from her neck and pressed a kiss to the tender skin below her ear. "Do you have a preference? Water? Juice? Beer?"

She stirred. "You have juice?"

"I'm not sure. I never know what's in my refrigerator. It's a surprise every time I open the door, but I'll go check."

She chuckled lightly. "Water or juice will be fine, but not beer. It's morning and the sun is definitely not over the yardarm, at least not in Texas."

"Good point." He blinked at the light streaming in through the tall windows. "I guess I sort of lost track of time." He dropped a light kiss to her ear. "I'll be right back."

The heat that had been like a blanket around her left with him. Yasmine stretched like a cat, then angled her head to glance out the nearest window. The morning light was bright and intense. It was time for her to leave.

Grimacing with regret and a slight soreness, she pushed herself up from the floor and reached for the T-shirt that lay in a heap beside Rio's jeans. They had both come off sometime during their lovemaking. She slipped the T-shirt on just as Rio sauntered back into the room.

"Here you go," he said without the slightest hint of embarrassment that he was naked.

And why should he be embarrassed? she thought. When two people had shared the intimacies they'd shared, it was ridiculous to feel even the least bit uncomfortable in the other's presence, whether you were dressed or not. However, she was very glad the T-shirt at least partially covered her. Her recent discovery that she loved him had left her feeling vulnerable enough without standing naked in front of him.

He held up two cans of soda. "Breakfast in a can. Caffeine to wake you up, calories to get you going, and liquid to sate your thirst. You just can't beat it."

She had to grin. "Typical male thinking."

"Right-on-*target* male thinking," he said. He handed her one of the sodas, took a long swig from the other, then gestured toward her with the can. "You're dressed?"

"It's morning."

"Yeah, so you said before."

"I just assumed you would want to get to work. I mean, when I showed up last night, I interrupted you."

"Work." His gaze shot to his computer, then back at her. His eyes had turned icy and his easygoing demeanor had disappeared.

"I didn't look at it, Rio. I was tempted, but I didn't."

"Are you sure you didn't?"

His distrust of her was a stab straight through her heart. Suddenly the morning light felt cold around her, seemed hard and sharp against her skin, was harsh and cruel against her eyes. Protectively she wrapped her arms around her waist and tightly held herself.

She knew her reaction was personal and totally inappropriate to what was a purely business matter. She knew that Rio, plainly a master at compartmentalization, viewed her in two ways: as a woman with whom he'd just shared a wild night of sex, and as a competitor trying to buy his company. She knew love didn't enter the picture for him as it did for her. She knew all of that and she still hurt.

"I'm positive," she said after a moment. "As I said, I was tempted—who in my position wouldn't have been?—but it wouldn't have been ethical for me to look."

"Ethical." His gaze was brooding and intense as he stared at her.

Watching him, Yasmine could practically see the wheels turning in his head. Somehow she knew he believed her, but something she'd said had set his mind spinning off in a different direction. She wished she knew what that direction was.

"Right," he finally said. "Ethical—a trait that's become something of a rarity these days." He took a long drink from his soda. "Word is you're something of a computer whiz."

She shrugged, tension and hurt still running through her body in almost intolerable measures. "I'm not in your league, but then, I don't know anyone who is."

He slowly smiled. "You're very good for my ego."

He was standing in front of her naked, looking and smelling like pure sex, and they were talking about business. She hated it, hated it fervently. "You know how good you are, Rio," she said, coolness creeping into her voice despite her attempt to keep it bland. "You don't need me or anyone else telling you."

"I guess you missed my original point," he drawled, his expression sharpening. "It was that if you'd looked at my computer, you would have understood what you were seeing."

She nodded. "More than likely."

"Yasmine," he said softly, forcefully. "What's on that computer is not only my business and my income, it's my reputation. Hell, it's my future."

Her brows drew together in a frown. "I understand that."

He reached for his jeans, jerked them on, and yanked up the zipper. "I don't see how you could."

Yasmine felt as if he'd kicked her. Her cheeks flamed, and she abruptly turned away.

From Rio's point of view, everything he'd just said pointed at the differences between them and the reason he'd probably never trust her, no matter how many times she proved herself to him. Unlike him, her income, her reputation, her future were all secure simply because of her last name. She didn't believe he begrudged her for it, but quite obviously he distrusted her because of it.

She wasn't sure what Rio's intent had been, but all at once a wave of helplessness swept over her. There were a lot of things in the world she could change, but her last name was not one of them.

"Look, I need to get dressed and get back over to Rachel and Brent's before they put out a missing person's report on me."

Rachel knew exactly where she was, Yasmine reflected, but she needed an excuse to leave, because suddenly she wanted nothing more than to get as far away from Rio as possible. But as she moved past him, heading for the stairs, he caught her arm.

"I'm sorry," he said.

"Why?" she asked, her voice wavering, but her gaze locked steadily on his. "You were telling it as you see it."

She wrenched her arm from his and hurried up the stairs. In his bedroom she snatched up her clothes from the floor and went into the bathroom to put them on. But once there, she suddenly stopped.

What was she doing?

She'd be *damned* if she was going to leave Rio's home in a rush, looking and feeling like a wreck with her hair tangled and disordered, her clothes disheveled, her bra strap dangling from her purse.

She knew she meant nothing more to Rio than a one-night stand, but she was too proud to slink away as if she had done something to be ashamed of.

EIGHT

In the shower, the warm water pulsed over her from a shower head installed higher than normal to accommodate Rio's height. It was like being in the rain, she thought, leaning tiredly against the tile wall, her eyes closed.

The water soaked her hair and sluiced down her body, soothing the soreness from her muscles and washing away the scent of hours of lovemaking. But she knew that she'd always be able to conjure up the scent. And she knew she'd never want to forget it.

The shower door opened and Rio stepped in. She'd expected him.

He threaded his fingers through her wet hair and angled her head so that he could gaze deeply into her eyes. "You haven't left yet and I'm already missing you. When am I going to see you again?"

She cleared her throat. "I—I don't know." She

wasn't certain she could be with him again without giving away everything to him—her anger, her hurt, and most especially her love—and she couldn't risk it. As long as she held on to those things, she'd be able to hold on to her pride, and right now with her heart in shreds and her emotions in turmoil, her pride was about all she had left.

"I'm not sure I can get through the day without you," he muttered.

He was serious, she realized, and understood perfectly. He'd had her and he wanted her again, and the same went for her. Unfortunately, it wasn't that simple for them.

She pushed past him and out of the shower, seized the first towel she saw, and wrapped it around her. Then, her clothes firmly in her grasp, she walked into the bedroom, where there was more space. But she could still see him standing in the bathroom. "Have you been thinking about my offer?" Bringing up the offer was the one thing she knew would push all sensual thoughts from his head.

"I've been kind of busy with you," he said, jerking a towel off the rack and following her into the bedroom, dripping wet.

Averting her gaze from his naked body, she quickly dressed.

"But I will think about it," he said as he absently dried himself.

Something in his voice made her look at him,

and she saw that his expression was thoughtful and troubled. She wished she'd never made the offer, but she had, and the sooner it was settled, the better it would be for everyone. "Fine. But I would appreciate your response in a few days. Wyatt and I have a couple of other things going."

"Sure."

Yasmine stepped out of Rachel and Brent's house and onto the back terrace. The sun had dried all traces of the previous night's rain, and shone brightly on the vivid green lawn. Beyond, in the meadow, bluebonnets and Indian paintbrush had been coaxed to life.

Rachel lounged in a pillowed chair, a knitting basket with blue yarn on her left and a second knitting basket with pink yarn on her right. She was knitting up a storm with the blue yarn. Her face, Yasmine reflected with amusement, also resembled a storm.

Buster immediately sprang up from his position at his mistress's side and ecstatically loped over to greet Yasmine. His tail swished back and forth with excitement.

"Good morning, Buster." Yasmine bent to give him a pat and scratch behind his ears. "Good morning, Rachel."

"Morning?" Rachel glanced vaguely toward the sky. "Yes, yes, well, I do declare, it *is* morning, isn't it? My, how time flies when you're worried sick about a friend."

"You were worried?" Yasmine moved toward a table that held coffee and muffins, and Buster trotted along behind her.

"Worried? Me? Why would I be worried?" Rachel put aside the blue yarn and reached for the pink. "I mean, just because I have a friend who doesn't think it's important to call and check in and let me know that she's safe and isn't lying by the road somewhere, a victim of a car wreck or a serial killer, is no reason for me to be worried—right?"

"You left out a possible attack by the Loch Ness monster," Yasmine drawled.

"The Loch Ness monster?"

"Well, they can't seem to find him in Loch Ness, now, can they?" She held up a muffin. "Are these orange muffins any good?"

"No, they can't, and yes, they're delicious." Rachel thrust aside her knitting and fixed her with a stern gaze. "Why didn't you at *least* give me a call?"

"You knew where I was." Yasmine settled herself in a cushioned glider with her muffins and coffee. Buster positioned himself in front of her with a hopeful gaze.

"Yeah, I knew where you were, but a person still worries, you know. Especially a *pregnant* person whose hormones are going *ballistic* all the time."

"Oh, come on, Rach." Yasmine tossed one of the muffins to Buster. "You weren't worried—you were *curious* and you wanted to know what was going on."

Rachel shrugged and the corners of her mouth turned up in a broad smile. "It would have been nice of you, thoughtful even, to have called me every so often. I didn't expect much, just a little report now and then, giving me all the juicy details."

Yasmine sipped her coffee and munched on her muffin. "Have you considered that most reasonable, logical people would have deduced that the very *lack* of a report was a report in and of itself?"

Rachel leaned forward. "Didn't you just hear me say that I'm *pregnant*? I don't have one brain cell of reason and logic left in my entire head."

"Okay, okay—calm yourself. Here's the story. I took the two baskets of food over to Rio's last night, even got the tablecloth and the candles on the table, but we never got around to eating any of the food, nor did we think to put any of it in the refrigerator."

Rachel stared at her, transfixed. "Yeah? And so?"

And the last time they'd made love, they'd done so without a condom. . . . "And so we had to throw out all the perishables this morning."

"*Yasmine Marie Elizabeth Damaron*, you really are being infuriating!"

She stood and threw Buster the remains of her orange muffin. "I'm sorry, sweetie, but I'm really tired and I need a nap in the worst way."

"A nap? *Now?* But what about the *details*?"

Yasmine chuckled. "Think about it, Rach. I just gave you as many details as you gave me after your first date with Brent."

"Yasmine, my darling, my best friend in the whole wide world, I want you to know that you are under absolutely *no* obligation to emulate my past high standards. In fact, I would think *less* of you if you didn't share everything, and I do mean everything."

With a grin, Yasmine selected another orange muffin, walked over to Rachel, and dropped a kiss on her forehead. "No way."

Rachel exhaled a long-suffering breath. "Oh, all right, you don't have to hit me over the head. I can take a hint. You don't want to tell me anything, and heaven knows, I've never been one to pry."

"Uh-huh." Yasmine straightened. "I love you, sweetie."

"I love you too."

"And listen, as for what happened last night—I need to think about some things, get them straight in my mind, and I need to do it by myself."

"As much as I hate to admit it, I do understand. I really do." Rachel glanced at the pink yarn, then the blue yarn, then the pink yarn again. "I think I'll go take a nap too." She held out her hand to Yasmine. "Could you please help me up?"

A frown wrinkled Yasmine's forehead as she pulled her out of the chair. "Isn't it a little early in the day for you to have a nap?"

Rachel grimaced. "You weren't the only one

who didn't get much sleep last night, though I'm certain you had much more fun than I did. My little one was doing pas de chat *and* playing football in my stomach all night long. Oh, by the way, I may not be here this afternoon when you wake up. I've got a doctor's appointment."

"Why?" Yasmine took a closer look at her friend. "Are you all right?"

"The appointment is strictly routine. Trust me, I'm as healthy as a horse. Or as healthy as I can be carrying around a fifty-pound watermelon in my stomach twenty-four hours a day."

Yasmine chuckled. "There's no way you've gained fifty pounds."

"I was being kind to myself. It feels more like sixty pounds at the very least. I can't *believe* the weight I'm putting on."

Yasmine leaned toward her to give her a hug. "Rachel, I don't care how much weight you've gained, I've never in my entire life seen a more beautiful pregnant lady than you."

Rachel gave her a teary smile. "I knew there was some reason I chose you as my best friend back in the fifth grade."

Yasmine laughed. "Actually, honey, I chose you. And by the way, tell your doctor I will pay big bucks to know the sex of my godchild."

Penny perched on the edge of Rio's desk. "Hey, boss."

His gaze held steady on the computer screen. "What's up?"

"You tell me. I put Tex Camden's call through ten minutes ago, and the light on your line went out two minutes after that. Since you haven't buzzed me, I figured you must have gotten bad news, but I came to check anyway."

"Bad news," he said, nodding. "And the decision is definite." Tearing his attention away from the monitor, he swung his chair around and looked at her. "Camden was all apologies. He hoped this wouldn't affect our working together on my banking needs in the future, but a loan at this time, especially as quickly as I need it and in the amount I need, is simply not feasible."

"But why?" she asked. "Was it the two missing board members?"

Today, metallic green striped Penny's hair and covered her nails, and a green of only a degree less intensity colored her skirt and T-shirt. Penny was back to her usual flamboyant style, and all was right with the world. Or, Rio amended grimly, as it should be.

He picked up a pencil and drummed it against his knee in time with the rock music blaring from the other room. "Camden was finally able to get in touch with both members, but apparently the one who's in Africa on safari wasn't a bit pleased about his vacation being interrupted by a phone call. That or he was just in an extremely bad mood, because *he* was the one who nixed the deal."

"The creep!" Penny said darkly. "I hope he finds out firsthand what the term *man-eating tiger* means."

Rio raked his fingers through his hair. "It's my fault, Penny. I got too involved with Tsunami and waited too damn long to start this." A wave of his hand indicated the code on his monitor screen.

She pointed one green-tipped finger at him. "Don't you dare blame yourself. There's not a one of us here who doesn't know what Tsunami means to you and will mean to all of us when it comes out."

"But Tsunami is not going to pay the bills anytime soon."

"I know, Rio, but this is all going to work out. I know it will. And if it comes to it, I'll work without a paycheck."

A lump rose in his throat, but he managed to eye her levelly. "No, Penny, you won't, because I won't let you, and that goes for everyone else too."

"Actually, Rio, if that time comes, you really won't have anything to say about it—"

"The hell I won't."

She held up a hand. "But we're not there yet, so we're not going to argue about it now."

He shook his head and drew in a deep breath. "I'll tell you where we *are*. I'm seriously considering taking the Damaron offer."

"*What?*"

He shrugged. "It would solve a lot of problems and make a lot of people happy."

"But not you."

"No, not me."

"Then wait. You don't have to make your decision today."

"I may have already waited too long. Tomorrow, at the latest, I'm going to have to call Borggeo-Wagner and let them know their product won't be coming in on time. I'll also have to tell them I have no idea when it *will* come in. And if they pull the contract, as they'll have every right to do, it'll leave us dead in the water."

"They won't pull it."

He rubbed the side of his face and realized he'd forgotten to shave that morning. But with Yasmine in his shower, he'd been thinking of other things. "Hell, I'd pull the contract if I were them."

"*Stop.*" She held out her hand, palm toward him like an old-fashioned traffic cop. "No more negative vibes, you hear? From this point forward, only *positive* thoughts. The Damaron offer was made days ago, but up until today you haven't seriously thought about it. Give yourself more time, Rio—a day or two more at the very least." She pushed away from his desk. "By the way, I'm glad you decided to work at home last night. You look more rested today than I've seen you look in a long while."

He grinned crookedly. "I am feeling better, but I wouldn't say I'm any more rested."

"*Really?*" Penny asked, pausing in the doorway.

"That sounds interesting. Want to tell me about it?"

"Want to tell me about what you and Michael did last night?"

"Point taken," she said with a laugh and a casual wave.

He swiveled back to face the computer, but instead of seeing the code on the monitor, he saw Yasmine's beautiful face, exactly what he'd been seeing ever since she'd left his house that morning. Damn, but he wished he were with her right this minute.

The night they'd shared had been amazing. *She'd* been amazing. Together they had been *beyond* amazing.

He was unaccustomed to wanting a woman as much as he'd wanted Yasmine last night. He was unaccustomed to thinking about a woman during the day, when he should be working. He was unaccustomed to wishing he were still with a woman after a night of lovemaking.

Yet with Yasmine it was all true.

But then, he'd known from the first that Yasmine was unlike any other woman. His work had always been his one and only obsession, the one thing he thought about night and day, the one thing he poured himself into body and soul.

But now his obsession with Yasmine was coming perilously close to equaling his obsession for his work. Luckily he was pretty sure he'd figured out why.

He and Yasmine had only a short time together, so naturally the impact of anything said or felt during that time was magnified. In addition, his business troubles, along with his determination to keep his company, clashed violently with her equally determined effort to buy his company. Nerves and emotions were heightened and intensified on both sides.

The strong feelings that ran between them wouldn't last. One way or another, her offer would be resolved and she would leave his life. Even if he were left with no other choice but to accept her offer, she wouldn't be involved in the day-to-day activities of running his company. Yasmine was a Damaron, which meant she worked and lived on a whole different level from his.

Fires, no matter how big, eventually burned out. Yasmine would leave, and they would never meet again. His obsession would fade.

The only thing left for him to do now was to decide whether or not to accept the offer.

Taking it *would* solve a great many problems. Yasmine would get his company, which would make her happy. He'd have enough money to finish the Borggeo-Wagner contract and get Tsunami launched in a major way, which would make him very happy. The method of getting the money, however, would definitely *not* make him happy.

He glanced up at the picture of his grandfather standing in front of his first oil well, a look of elation on his face. He understood his grandfather's joy, because he'd felt the very same emotion as he'd built his company, project by successful project. In the end his grandfather had nothing and people had been hurt. His own dad, for instance, because he'd never understood his father's penchant for gambling everything on a single sinking of a drill deep into the earth.

Now Rio was more or less in the same situation, and God knew, he didn't want to hurt his father. He also didn't want to hurt the people who worked for him and depended on him. He once again rubbed the side of his face. Yes, it would definitely make a lot of people happy if he took the Damaron offer.

And there was one more plus to taking the offer. Yasmine would never have to know that he'd lied to her when he'd made their deal and had said he'd think about the offer. Amazingly enough, of all the reasons he had for taking the offer, the last seemed the most important to him.

He glanced at the phone, wondering what she was doing at this precise moment, wondering if she was thinking about last night as he was, if she was thinking about him. . . .

Dammit! Thinking about Yasmine wasn't getting the job done.

He drew in a deep breath, slowly exhaled it, and forced his concentration back to the computer screen. After a few moments of thought, he cursed again, then quickly typed a series of commands into the computer that erased everything he'd done so far on the Borggeo-Wagner project.

Yasmine came slowly awake a little before noon and for a moment felt disoriented.

Rio. His name, his image, instantly came to her. She'd fallen asleep thinking about him and she'd awakened thinking about him. She supposed it was only natural, since she was in love with him.

He had her heart though he hadn't asked for it, didn't want it, and would be stunned if he knew. She was stunned herself, stunned that she hadn't guarded her heart more.

Then again, she'd never really had a chance.

Falling in love with Rio was the second biggest surprise of her life, and because of it, she was already in pain.

Rio didn't love her.

If only they could have met under more normal circumstances without the complication of the DI offer between them. But it had been *because* of the offer, she reminded herself, that they'd met at all. Unfortunately the offer was still there between them like a treacherous, incredibly high mountain, impossible to climb, to go through, or to even get around.

She stretched, and sore muscles all over her body protested, the result of her vigorous activities of the night. Her body had adapted to his so easily, in fact had flourished with his attention, but it was a new day now and she had to deal with the aftermath of those hours of ecstasy.

Somewhat gingerly, she rolled off the bed and went into the bathroom to wash her face. She returned to the bedroom and sat down on the edge of the bed to continue trying to think it all through.

She now knew Rio well enough to realize that she could quadruple her offer and he still would not take it, not unless his back was to the wall and he had no other alternative. And if he did have to sell, he would always view the buyer of his company as someone who had taken his baby away from him, even though that was far from what Damaron International wanted or intended.

She also knew that in the end, the only reason he'd said he would think about her offer was that he was having financial problems. But why was he in that position in the first place? The Borggeo-Wagner contract was all she could think of that might be giving him trouble. But given time, she knew he'd figure out the problem. Given time, he'd get himself out of his financial crunch. Given time . . .

She hit the flat of her hand against her forehead. *She'd been had and in more ways than one.*

Time was what he needed, and it was exactly what she'd given him. Now she understood that the most important part of their deal was the one part she'd overlooked.

He'd wanted her to stop Wyatt's investigation, because if Wyatt had continued, word would have gotten out, and Rio would have risked losing the one thing that would sustain his company through a crisis—his reputation.

It wasn't in his makeup to consider selling his baby unless he had no other choice. He would play out all his options until the very end.

In a way he'd played fair with her by telling her exactly what he needed. In another way he hadn't played fair, because she was certain he'd had no intention at the time of looking seriously at their offer.

Dammit. Why did she have to go and fall in love with such a stubborn, independent man? More than that, why did she have to go and fall in love with probably the *one* man in the entire world who didn't care who or what she was or how much money she could give him?

With a heavy sigh, she reached for the phone and punched out Wyatt's number.

NINE

"I don't get it." Rio gazed at Penny, his expression completely bewildered, his hand still clutching the phone's receiver he'd hung up only moments before. "That was Tex Camden. He said the money for my loan will be in my business account by the end of today. All I have to do is drive over and sign the papers."

"Wow." Penny dropped dazedly into a chair. "Wow."

Rio shook his head. "When I asked what had happened since this morning to make him change his mind, he simply said circumstances had altered."

"Maybe the board member who's in Africa got hold of some sort of happy juice."

Rio grinned at Penny's fiendish tone. "Maybe. Camden didn't elaborate, and I didn't push. In fact, he offered me such good terms, about all I could do was accept and say thanks."

Recovered from her shock, Penny clapped her hands together with excitement. "Well, *okay*. See— I told you things would work out."

"Yes, you did. And it's better than you know. This morning I trashed the code for the Borggeo-Wagner contract and started over."

She eyed him uncertainly. "And that's good?"

He smiled. "It's very good. I should have done it days ago. I'd coded myself into a corner, but I couldn't see it. My mind was going in ten different directions and I couldn't focus. But I just kept thinking that if I worked at it long enough . . ." He shrugged. "Well, anyway, I'm making a run at the problem in a different way."

"And you think you're finally on the right track?"

"I don't know for sure, but yeah, I do think I am. An hour or two more of work and I should know for sure."

"That's absolutely terrific." Penny jumped up from her seat. "I tell you what. To save you time, I'll drive over to the bank, get the papers, bring them back here for your signature, and then return them."

He nodded. "That would be a big help. Thank you. By the time you get back, I'll—"

"Oh, hi, Yasmine," Penny said brightly.

Rio whirled his chair around, and a thunderbolt of electricity jolted through him at the sight of Yasmine. With a slow, intimate smile, he leaned back in his chair. "Let me guess. You don't have an appointment."

She shook her head. "No, I don't."

"Not that you need one," Penny said as she passed Yasmine on her way out of the office. "At least not today. Go on in. He's in a good mood."

"She's right," he said, still smiling. "I'm in an excellent mood. Come in and shut the door."

"Thank you," she murmured.

He stood and started toward her, but Yasmine ducked around him and took the chair beside his desk.

He shut the door, then turned back to her. She was wearing a cream-colored sleeveless dress with gold at her ears and throat, and a golden ribbon entwined in her topaz braid. As always, she shimmered and gleamed. As always, she took his breath away.

Having the loan approved had made him happy. Getting onto the right track with the code had made him even happier. But seeing Yasmine again was making him close to ecstatic. "Last night and this morning have a great deal to do with my excellent mood," he said huskily. "In fact, I had planned to call you in a little while."

She lifted her head and looked up at him, her face without expression. "I came to tell you I'm leaving."

Her announcement threw him. He'd been so

happy to see her that he must have missed a signal. "Pardon me?"

"I'm leaving, probably first thing in the morning."

He walked toward her, tense and thoroughly confused. "Why?"

She shrugged. "I'd planned to be here only a week anyway. The main thing is, I won't be pestering you anymore."

"Pestering me?" He was hearing her words, but he wasn't understanding them. "What are you talking about?"

"I'm talking about the offer. A short time ago I called Wyatt and told him that I had decided to officially withdraw the offer."

All he wanted to do was grab her to him and kiss her, but he knew from experience that once he started kissing her, it was very hard to stop. Besides, her mystifyingly distant demeanor was telling him she wouldn't welcome so much as a touch of his hand on her skin. He folded his arms across his chest. "Yasmine," he said, his voice quiet and controlled, "as you once said to me, that doesn't make sense."

"And as you once said to me, it doesn't have to make sense to you, only to me."

"And as I recall, it didn't matter what I said. You stood your ground and argued tooth and nail that you *needed* it to make sense to you."

"Is that what you're going to do? Argue with me?"

Emotion finally showed on her face, and to his surprise, the emotion was wariness. Something else that didn't make sense. After what he'd said to her the night before, he would have expected anger. "Would last night have anything to do with all of this?"

"No, not at all. This is purely business."

"Business, huh?" Skepticism thickened his voice.

"At any rate, what possible difference does it make what the reason is, Rio? You didn't want our deal in the first place."

"No, you're right, I didn't. But would you believe I came extremely close to calling and accepting your offer earlier today?"

"No, I wouldn't."

The somber tone of her voice made his head snap back. "What's going on here, Yasmine?"

"I told you. I'm officially withdrawing the offer."

"Okay," he said slowly. "That's fine. I never wanted your offer, and as it now happens, I don't need it."

"Then everything worked out all the way around." She stood. "Good-bye, Rio."

"Wait a minute." He couldn't believe that she intended to walk out of his life as if there'd never been anything between them. "What about last night?"

His sharp voice stopped her halfway across the

room, and she turned back to him. "It shouldn't have happened."

"But it did. And in case you've forgotten, it was *you* who came to *me*."

She showed no reaction, and he suddenly realized with a start that she hadn't once reached for her ribbon. Something was wrong here. But what?

"I haven't forgotten," she said evenly. "But we both know it was nothing more to you than a distraction, so why even bring it up?"

He let out a string of curses. "To *hell* with anything being a distraction. Last night was nothing short of sensational."

Leaving Rio and making him believe that she didn't care about him one way or the other was the hardest thing she'd ever had to do, Yasmine reflected with sorrow. In fact, she was having to battle herself so that the effort she was making wouldn't show. Unfortunately the battle had begun to take a heavy toll on her. She was shaking inside. "Yes," she said as calmly as possible, "but once again, why bring it up? You know that our relationship can't possibly go anywhere."

"And why's that, exactly?" he asked in a sarcastic drawl, his eyes diamond hard. "Because you're a high-and-mighty Damaron who views people as pawns to be used?"

She almost laughed. He was accusing her of using him, when it had been he who had used her. As a form of self-defense, she deliberately infused a tone of cruelty into her voice. "What did you expect, Rio? That we'd continue on as lovers until one of us got tired of the other?"

He shifted his stance and distractedly ran a hand through his hair. "What's wrong with that?"

"Nothing, I suppose. And that's the way it works a lot of times, but it's not feasible for me. My life is much too hectic. I never know where I'm going to be from one day to the next."

"Packed social schedule, huh?"

"Pretty much."

"Dammit, Yasmine." A vein stood out on his forehead. "After last night, you can't make me believe you can just walk away without having at least a few feelings tug at you."

For the first time, hope began to flutter in her breast. "Why, Rio?"

"Why what?"

"Why do you think that I shouldn't be able to just walk away, fancy-free, without another thought? We've both agreed that last night was sensational, but it was just sex, right?" He seemed lost for words, and her hope grew. "Or do you think there was more?"

He stared at her, perplexed. "You're talking about love, aren't you?"

His baffled tone left no doubt that the thought of love had not occurred to him before then, and her hopes plummeted.

"You know, Rio," she said, the softness of her voice covering her hurt, "with you and me, sex and business always seem to get tangled up together.

Lines blur and we forget the real issue we should be concentrating on."

"*The damn offer.*" He practically spat out the words.

She nodded coolly. If she were an actress, she thought, she'd win an Academy Award for this performance. "The original reason I came here was to make you the offer. The reason I'm leaving now is that I've withdrawn the offer. I'm sure you'll agree that everything in between was incidental and accidental. And as for the reason I've withdrawn the offer—if I've learned nothing else about you, Rio, I've learned that no matter what, you'll always go your own way. You wouldn't be able to stand working under anyone else, no matter how much autonomy you were given. Good-bye."

"We didn't use a condom the last time we had sex."

She'd almost reached the door when his words stopped her. He'd thrown them at her as if they were knives and she felt as if each one of them had pierced her heart. For a moment she was afraid her legs would give way beneath her. She didn't even trust herself to be able to turn, so instead she glanced at him over her shoulder. "I know we didn't, but you've got nothing to worry about. It's the wrong time of month for me to be fertile."

"There are children all over the world whose mothers said the very same thing. Besides, who said I was worried?"

Her hand closed around the doorknob, but before she could open the door, he said, "There's one more thing."

If she didn't get out of there soon, she was going to break apart and start to cry, something she vehemently did not want to do in front of him. "What is it?" she asked, this time without looking at him.

"I lied to you about the deal I made with you," he said, his tone solemn. "I never had any intention of seriously considering your offer."

"I know," she said, then opened the door and left.

Rio leaned back in his chair and closed his eyes. Rock music and laughter blared from the next room. He finally had the code he needed to fulfill the Borggeo-Wagner contract, and with the loan and the final payment from Borggeo-Wagner, he would have enough money to see Tsunami through to its launch. He should be on top of the world, but he wasn't. Something was wrong. Something was *very* wrong.

He pressed his thumb and forefinger against his eyelids. It didn't make sense to him that Yasmine would so suddenly and unexpectedly give up on trying to get him to accept DI's offer. Before today, she'd been so incredibly determined and persistent. No, it didn't make sense.

It was as if the two of them had been in the center of a violent storm together and then suddenly, abruptly, the booming thunder had quieted, the lightning had halted mid-flash, suspended in the sky, and the roar of the wind had ceased until not even the lightest of leaves stirred.

It wasn't natural. It didn't make sense.

His private line rang. Normally he wouldn't have answered it, but he was so off balance, he found himself picking it up before he realized what he was doing. "Yes?"

"Rio, it's your father."

His father always identified himself, Rio thought wryly, as if he thought his son wouldn't recognize his voice. "Hi, Dad." Since his dad called him so rarely, he added. "What's up?"

"Nothing much. It's your mother, you know. She tends to get worried, so she wanted me to call you."

"About what?"

"Oh, I just had a little episode with my heart the other night."

Rio's hands tightened around the receiver. "Your heart? *When?*"

"Two nights ago. Your mother insisted on calling the paramedics and they came and took me off to the hospital. I could have driven myself to the hospital. I also could have gone home that same night, and I *told* them so too, but the doctors insisted I should stay there for a couple of days so they could run their tests and at the same time run up my bill—you know how they are. I'm home now though. Got home yesterday, and everything's fine."

Rio was stunned. "You were in the hospital for two days and you didn't call and tell me?"

"Well, you know your mother, son. She didn't want you worried until we knew something for sure."

"Dad—" His instinct was to yell at his father for not telling him what had happened at the time it was happening. But he'd never in his life raised his voice to his father and he wasn't going to start now. Besides, nothing he could say would change what had already happened. "What was the diagnosis?"

"Nothing serious. Just a mild heart attack. They've given me a little pill to take every day, which I suppose won't be such a hardship. But they've also told me I'm going to have to start exercising and eating broccoli and vegetables and the like, and you know how much I've always hated broccoli."

No, as a matter of fact, he didn't know, Rio reflected grimly. "I'm coming over to see you."

"No, no, no—that's not necessary. I called only because . . . well, your mother, you know. She wanted me to tell you something."

"What is it?" The realization that he might have actually lost his father a few nights ago had him shaking.

"She . . . I . . . well, we wanted you to know, son, that this minor little setback of mine doesn't affect the offer I made you for that loan. In fact, it doesn't even have to be a loan. If you can, pay it back. If you can't, don't worry about it. But if you need it, we want you to have it."

Tears filled Rio's eyes, and he was so surprised that for a moment he wasn't sure what to do. Then he hastily brushed them away. "Dad, what time do you go to bed?" It was shocking for him to realize that he didn't even know his own father's routine. It was even more shocking that his father hadn't felt close enough to him to call when he'd had a heart attack.

"Usually right after the ten o'clock news. Why?"

"Because I'll be over tonight." He wanted to see with his own eyes that his father was all right, and he wanted to talk with his mother to find out exactly what the doctors had prescribed for his dad and what their prognosis for him was.

"Now, son—"

"I'll see you tonight, okay?"

"Well, all right, if you insist. You know how happy your mother will be to see you. In fact, why don't you come for dinner if you can? Your mother would love it."

"Fine, I'll be there. And, Dad? There's one more thing I want you to know." He drew in a deep breath and quickly exhaled it. "I love you."

There was stunned silence from the other end of the line, and he knew his father didn't have a clue what to say to him.

"See you tonight," Rio said gently, and hung up the phone.

There was one thing that was about to change for the better in his life, Rio thought with determination, and that was his relationship with his father. They'd missed too many years already.

"Here are the papers," Penny said, placing them in a clear space on his desk beside his computer. "Sign everywhere you see a big red X." She glanced over at him and suddenly frowned. "What's wrong?"

His face must still be registering his shock at the events that had occurred during the last hour, he reflected ruefully. "Yasmine came by—well, you saw her as you were leaving. Anyway, she came by to withdraw her offer and to say she was leaving town tomorrow. Then Dad called to say he'd had a *minor* heart attack two nights ago, had been in the hospital, but that he was home now and feeling fine."

"Wow."

He nodded his agreement. "Yeah. I'm going over to see him this evening just to make sure everything really is okay."

"Good," Penny said. "And let me know if there's anything I can do."

He smiled gratefully at her. He could always count on her. "I will. Thanks. But knowing Mom and Dad, they've already got everything organized."

Penny sat down. "As for Yasmine, you want to hear something odd?"

"Odd? About Yasmine?"

She nodded. "While I was waiting for the loan papers to be finished up, I had a nice chat with Camden's assistant, Sue. She and I went to high school together. Anyway, we were talking about hair and clothes and things like that and Sue happened to mention how elegant and beautiful she thought Yasmine Damaron had been when she'd come in earlier."

Rio stiffened. "Yasmine was at the bank today? Why?"

"That's exactly what I asked Sue, but as soon as I did, she got this horrified expression on her face like she'd said something she shouldn't and immediately clammed up."

Rio rocked back in his chair. "Get Camden on the phone for me."

"Guess what, Yasmine?" Rachel asked excitedly.

Sitting at the kitchen table, Yasmine tore her gaze away from the window and the patio beyond, where she and Rio had shared their first kiss, and she saw her friend lumbering into the kitchen, holding her stomach.

She took a sip from the cup of tea she'd prepared for herself. "Is this a guessing game?" she asked listlessly.

Rachel maneuvered herself into a chair across the table from Yasmine. "I can tell you're in a crummy mood and I'm positive it's got something to do with Rio, which you can tell me all about later. But right now I've got the *coolest* news you've ever heard in your life and I *guarantee* you that once you hear it, you'll snap right out of that wretched mood."

Yasmine propped her chin on her hand, trying to show interest, but her tone was decidedly lackluster. "Rachel, honey, *no* piece of news can be *that* good."

"Uh-huh, well, you just wait for it. Do you remember me telling you this morning that I had a doctor's appointment?"

Yasmine nodded, her interest gradually increasing. "Is everything okay?"

"If things were any better, I wouldn't be able to stand it. *Yaz!*" Rachel's eyes were wide and sparkling. "I'm going to have *twins!*"

"You're going to have what?" Yasmine asked blankly.

"*Twins!*"

Yasmine's hand fell away from her chin. "You're kidding me."

"No, I'm not kidding you, not even one little bit."

If someone could dance with delight while she

was sitting at a table, Yasmine thought, Rachel was doing it. "Well *tell* me—what, where, how, why."

Rachel took a deep breath, trying to calm herself down. "Because of the unusual amount of weight I've gained these last few weeks—" She stopped to shoot Yasmine a look. "See? I've been telling you I was a cow."

Yasmine threw up her hands. "Will you *please* get on with the story?"

"Okay, because of it, the doctor decided he should do a sonogram. Scared me half to death, because it wasn't scheduled, so I immediately called Brent and told him to hurry over. But when Brent arrived and the doctor fired up the machine . . ." Rachel's eyes teared. "There they were, Yaz—*two babies*."

"But—"

"Apparently one baby has been hiding behind the other all this time. Isn't that fabulous?"

Yasmine got up and hurried around the table to give Rachel a hug. "*Absolutely*, Rach. You were right. That's the best news I have *ever* heard." She straightened and ran a loving hand over Rachel's head. "I'm so happy for you."

"And there's even *more*," Rachel said, beaming.

"More? Wait a minute," she said dryly. "Maybe I should sit down again." She circled the table, dropped back into the chair, and spread her palms flat on the table. "Okay, I'm ready."

"I know the *sex* of the babies."

Yasmine's mouth dropped open. "You *don't*."

Rachel was so excited, she could barely sit still. "I *do*."

"How?"

"Well, the doctor knew we didn't want to know the sex, but we were practically in a catatonic state over the news about having twins, so the doctor was pointing out the babies and their various features to me and Brent, explaining everything so that we could understand how it could happen, and then, well, suddenly, we just couldn't mistake what we were seeing." She bobbed her head up and down in a nod. "The doctor said the evidence was pretty clear, and it was."

It was impossible for Yasmine to remain sad in the face of such miraculous news. The heaviness that had been weighing on her heart lifted. "Tell me, for goodness' sake. *Tell me*."

Rachel pounded her fists on the table in a fit of happiness. "You're just never going to *believe* it!"

"I won't unless you tell me," Yasmine said through gritted teeth.

Rachel squealed with delight. "We're going to have a *boy* and a *girl*. Now I understand why one day I would think I was having a boy and the next day I would be sure I was having a girl. Isn't this exciting?"

Yasmine's eyes filled with tears of happiness for Rachel. "I've never in my entire life heard anything more exciting," she said softly.

Dusk was settling over the meadow. The lake was shimmering a pearl-gray color. Yasmine pulled out her suitcase and began to pack, her heart once again heavy, her entire body filled with pain.

She and Rachel had spent a long time making plans for the babies, then she'd poured out her broken heart to Rachel, telling her all about her love for Rio and the reasons she had to leave. She'd probably be in pieces right now if she hadn't had that time with Rachel, she reflected ruefully. The excitement over the coming babies, combined with Rachel's love and good common sense, had helped her enormously.

She'd be all right, she told herself. Once she got home, she'd feel much better. People didn't *really* die of a broken heart.

She sank dejectedly down onto the bed. So then why, she wondered, was she feeling such unbearable pain?

A knock sounded on the door. "Come on in."

"Thank you."

With a gasp of surprise, she surged off the bed. "Rio!"

He strolled into the bedroom, looking agonizingly sexy and virile. He was wearing his usual faded jeans, but with a pressed black T-shirt and another beautifully cut sport jacket. She hadn't seen him dressed like that since the night of the party.

"What are you doing here?"

He strolled over to her suitcase, lifted out a lacy

bra, then dropped it and reached for a gold satin ribbon. "I came to try to talk you out of leaving."

"That's impossible."

"And if I can't do that," he continued as if she hadn't spoken, "there are still a few things I need to tell you and one thing in particular I would like to ask you."

His face was clean shaven, she noticed, and she could smell his fresh, masculine scent. "I think we've said quite enough to each other, Rio. Actually we've said more than we ever should."

Fingering the ribbon, he looked over at her. "We've said a lot to each other, Yasmine, but we haven't said it all. Not by any means. Would you please sit down and hear me out."

"This isn't a good idea," she said, knowing how fragile her composure was.

He held up his hands as if he were surrendering something to her. "I promise I'll leave after I've said my piece, if that's what you still want."

He had the golden ribbon wrapped around his fingers and when he'd held up his hands, the ribbon had draped down his forearm and was now clinging to his skin. "What do you mean, if that's what I still want?"

"There were no hidden meanings in what I just said, Yasmine, nor will there be in what I plan to say."

She heard his exceedingly gentle tone and for the first time noticed that his expression was grave. She didn't know what unnerved her more—his tone, his expression, or his fingers threaded with her satin ribbon.

With the hand that held the ribbon, he gestured toward the chair, making the ribbon ends flutter. "Please. I promise I won't keep you too long. I also promise I won't touch you if that's what you're worried about. All I want to do is talk to you."

She sighed, suddenly exhausted. Since she'd arrived in Texas, she had received one surprise after the other. She honestly didn't feel as if she could endure one more revelation, but it would probably take more energy than she had at the moment to get Rio to leave. She sat down in the armchair he'd indicated and waited for the next surprise, the next blow.

Rio sank onto the edge of the bed, and resting his forearms on his thighs, he leaned toward her. "I'm not a man who's ever been afraid of much of anything, Yasmine, but knowing you has taught me all about fear."

"Me?" she asked, startled.

He absently gathered up the ribbon and placed it in one hand, then clasped his fingers together so that he was cradling the ribbon between his two palms. "I couldn't figure it out either, but practically every time we were together, I'd feel this puzzling fear. Today I finally figured it out."

She suddenly nodded. "Oh, you mean you were afraid of the power I had to ruin your reputation."

"No, that's not what I'm talking about." A muscle moved along his jawline. "Yasmine, you've accused me of using you as a diversion—"

She stiffened. "I don't want to talk about that again."

He dropped his head for a moment. When he looked back at her, his eyes were glittering with the strength of some inner emotion she couldn't comprehend. "Let me just say this much: You were probably right, though it wasn't deliberate or conscious on my part. But on the other hand, my motives were far from pure."

She gave a sharp laugh that carried pain. "For once we agree on something."

He nodded. "Most of the time, I've been a first-class bastard to you, but you'll be glad to know that you've gotten me back."

She wrapped her arms around her waist. She didn't know where he was going, but she was pretty sure she was going to hate it. "I don't understand, Rio," she said without emotion. "But then, that's nothing new when I'm with you, so let's just call it quits while we're both ahead. Please leave now."

"I will in a moment," he said softly. "I promised you and I will. Right after I say that I finally realized the fear I've been feeling was because unconsciously I knew you were more than a distraction to me, *much* more. In fact, all this time I've been falling in love with you and I didn't even realize it until this afternoon."

Pain scored through her as she felt the color drain from her face. Slowly she shook her head.

"Don't, Rio. It's a cruel lie." Her brow wrinkled. "Why are you doing this? What do you want?"

His hands opened, the ribbon dangled from around one finger, and he reached toward her, but then just as quickly he pulled his hands back. "I'm not lying to you, Yasmine. I'm telling you the truth." He looked down at the ribbon. "I'd already admitted to myself that you were becoming an obsession to me, but I neatly explained it away. I decided you and I were all nerves and fire because of the intense situation we were in and that it would all go away once you left."

"It will," she said, her words sounding strangled. She wasn't sure how much more of this she could take.

"No, it won't, Yasmine. At least it won't for me. You see, I got hit squarely between the eyes today with a revelation. The president of my bank called to tell me that he had reversed his negative decision on a loan I badly needed and was going to give it to me after all. Then I discovered that you had paid him a visit earlier."

She'd let herself hope once already today. She wasn't going to do it again. "So?" she asked defiantly. "I was running a little low on cash and needed to cash a check."

"Maybe so. But while you were at it, you also put up the money for my loan. Money that came out of your own personal funds, money that had nothing whatsoever to do with DI."

"You weren't supposed to find any of that out,"

she said in a stunned whisper. "It was part of the agreement."

"Oh, it wasn't easy to get it out of ol' Tex. In fact, I couldn't do it over the phone. I had to go over and have a little talk with him, but I finally got enough out of him to put two and two together."

She wiped a hand across her brow, bracing herself. He was either about to go ballistic on her and throw the money back in her face, or he was going to try to smother her with gratitude. She'd hate it if he did either, which was why she hadn't wanted him to know it was her money.

She pushed up from the chair and quickly walked to the other side of the room. Only after she'd put the bed between them did she turn around again to give him a level look. "I'm sorry you found out, Rio. That was the last thing in the world I wanted. I realize it'll make it hard for you to accept the money, knowing it's coming from me, but please believe me, I did it only to help you, and there are absolutely *no* strings attached."

"I know," he said quietly, rising to face her. "I know." He gestured a little helplessly. "See, there I was this afternoon, pressure free for the first time in weeks. I knew there would be money coming in. I'd figured out the problem that was holding me up on the Borggeo-Wagner contract. I knew I could make the delivery to them within a short time." He spread out his hands. "I didn't have to pretend to anyone about anything. Normally under those circumstances, I would have thrown a party. But I couldn't, because I was hurting too much. You weren't there with me. You'd walked out of my life."

Yasmine took a step toward him, then realized what she was doing, and stopped. Her chest was tight. She wasn't even certain she was breathing. But she was listening—oh, *how* she was listening.

He didn't seem to notice what she'd done or was doing. He simply continued to finger the ribbon and kept talking. "I couldn't figure out why you'd withdrawn the offer and left so abruptly. And I couldn't figure out why I was hurting so damn much. And then I learned the loan had come from you." He gazed at her, his eyes glittering with warmth and truth. "You had potentially explosive knowledge that you could have used against me. It would have ruined me, and you probably would have ended up with what you came here for—my company. But you didn't. Instead, you gave me a gift with no strings or names attached to it so that I could have what *I* wanted."

Emotions jangled inside her until she couldn't hear herself think. So she decided to go cautiously with her instincts and say what she was feeling. "I didn't want you to lose your company."

He smiled at her. "I know, and once I realized that, it was pretty much a no-brainer for me. I had absolutely no more excuses to emotionally hold you at arm's length, and it was then the truth all came together. I love you, Yasmine. I love you. And I hope like hell that the gift you gave me means you love me too. That's one of the reasons I came here tonight—to find out."

She swallowed hard against a thick knot in her throat. "You love me?"

He nodded, his voice clogged with emotion. "Oh, yeah—you bet I do." His voice was soft as silk. "I've probably loved you since the day you first walked into my office, looking all golden and shimmering and businesslike." He moved his hand, and the ribbon slipped from his finger and drifted back into the suitcase, but he never stopped looking at her. "I'm sorry, Yasmine, for anything I've done to hurt you. All I can say is that I love you more than I ever thought it possible to love anyone, and if you love me even a little—or maybe even just like me some—I hope you'll stay and let me try to make the hurt up to you in whatever way I can. Maybe we could start all over again. Maybe—"

She'd heard enough. "I love you, Rio Thornton," she said, walking toward him. "I even *like* you." She reached him and slipped her arms around his neck and nestled her body close against his. "And yes, I'll stay for a while if you want."

"If I *want*?" he asked huskily, his eyes dark with fire, his tone and demeanor suddenly fierce and possessive. "Yasmine, if I told you all the things that I want from you, you might just run away in horror."

She threw back her head and laughed. "Try me."

The sound of her laugh, the feel of her in his

arms once again, were overwhelming. "I think I will," he said roughly, and lowered his mouth to hers.

Sometime later, Yasmine rose up on her elbow and looked around her. The suitcase had been kicked off the bed to the floor. Clothes were strewn everywhere. She turned her head and gazed lovingly down at Rio. "It appears you've unpacked for me."

He chuckled. "I don't like to waste time."

She grinned. "So I've noticed."

"*Time.*" With a sudden groan, Rio sat straight up in bed and looked at his watch. "Come on—we've still got plenty of time." He slid out of bed and started to dress quickly.

She sat up and pushed her hair away from her face. "Do you mind if I ask what you're talking about?"

A wry grin crept across his mouth. "I didn't ask you, did I? Remember when I first got here and I said there was one thing in particular I'd like to ask you?"

She waved her hand in a small circle. "Vaguely."

He returned to the bed and sat down beside her. "I would like to ask you if you would please come with me tonight to my parents' home for dinner."

"Dinner at your parents' home?" she asked,

both bemused and charmed. "I'd like that very much. And during dinner I can tell your father all about how wonderful you are."

"My parents are going to absolutely love you."

"Great," she said, maneuvering around him, her heart feeling as if it would burst with happiness. "Let's get going."

He caught her arm before she could slip off the bed. "There's just one more thing."

"What's that?" she asked, reflecting that she now knew how Rachel had felt when she'd been sitting still, yet at the same time dancing with happiness.

"Would you please wear your hair braided with one of your ribbons tonight?"

"If you'd like."

His eyes glinted. "I'd like that very much, so that all during dinner while you're talking to my father, I can plan how I'm going to take it out of your hair when I get you home with me."

Her gaze narrowed on him. "Don't you *dare*. I won't be able to concentrate."

He skimmed his finger along her bare shoulder. "Okay, but after we get back to my place, there's one more question I need to ask you, and I'll warn you right now, it has a great deal more to do with your future than my previous question about dinner tonight."

She shifted toward him and put her hands around his neck. "There's something you should know about me, Rio," she said. "I *hate* surprises, so ask me the question now."

"Gladly," he said huskily, taking one of her hands in his. "Will you marry me, Yasmine Damaron? Will you live with me forever and be my wife?"

"Yes," she said, her eyes shimmering with love. "I most definitely will."

THE EDITORS' CORNER

Hey! Look out your window. What do you see? Summer's finally in full bloom! And what does that mean? It means you can grab your four new LOVE-SWEPTs and head outdoors to read them! So when you're at the beach, in the backyard, or sitting on the dock of the bay, take care not to get sunburned while you bask in the warm summer sun reading your LOVESWEPTs!

Remember Georgia DeWitt, the woman who was jilted at the altar in DADDY MATERIAL? Well, she's back in **GEORGIA ON HIS MIND**, LOVE-SWEPT #842, Marcia Evanick's second chapter of her White Lace & Promises trilogy. Carpenter Levi Horst knows he has no business fantasizing about a woman who's clearly out of his league, especially when she's his boss! Georgia knows she doesn't inspire men to move mountains—her last experience taught her that. But when she sets up her own antiques business and discovers a kindred spirit who shares her secret dreams, she's forced to reconsider. Now all she has to do is convince Levi that they really aren't from two different worlds after all. In a story sparkling with wit and tender sensuality, Marcia tells us what can happen when two unlikely lovers are astonished by their heart's desires and decide to risk it all to become a family.

In **TRUST ME ON THIS,** LOVESWEPT #843 from award-winning Jennifer Crusie, con-buster Alec Prentice and reporter Dennie Banks are thrown together by a whim of fate, but both have their own agendas in mind. After Alec is convinced that Dennie is not in cahoots with a notorious con man, he enlists her help in trapping his quarry. Dennie wants to interview a woman for a story that's guaranteed to earn her the promotion she so richly deserves—and she'll do anything to get it. After offending the woman she was supposed to interview, Dennie thinks it's time for plan B. Enter Alec, who has promised to help if she'll agree to his terms. Can these two passionate partners in crime get their man *and* each other? (Of course they can, it's a LOVESWEPT!) But *how* they do it is another thing. Find out how in Jennifer Crusie's hilarious and fast-paced gem of a love story!

Got a fire extinguisher? Looks like Jack Riley and Mary Jo Simpson are gonna need it when they meet in a classic case of **SPONTANEOUS COMBUSTION,** LOVESWEPT #844. Mary Jo seems to need a hero, but even after Jack has fought through fire to rescue her, he still insists he's no hero. She trembles at his touch, a touch that thrills her no end. But it scares her even more. She's lost every man she's ever loved to the line of duty and fears this man will be no different. When she becomes Jack's prime suspect in an arson investigation, Jack must decide if trusting his mystery lady could mean getting burned. LOVE-SWEPT favorite Janis Reams Hudson returns in a steamy saga of a man and a woman torn between their desire to do what's right and their desire for each other.

Nicole Sanders would rather get stuck in the mud than jump into the car with sexy stranger Alex Coleman in **TELL ME NO LIES**, LOVESWEPT #845 by rising star Jill Shalvis. Alone for most of her life, Nicole is bewildered to learn that she's been purposely denied the one thing she wants most—family. Now she has to wade through a sea of lies that will ultimately force her to make the hardest decision of her life. Alex has always been a sucker for a damsel in distress, and Nicole is no exception. As he fights the walls around her soul, the key to her identity may be all that stands between a future of love and a past full of sorrow and bitterness. In a powerful story of longing and belonging, Jill Shalvis entangles a woman desperate for love with a man who promises to be all the family she'll ever need.

Happy reading!

With warmest wishes,

Shauna Summers *Joy Abella*

Shauna Summers   Joy Abella
Editor   Administrative Editor

P.S. Look for these Bantam women's fiction titles coming in July. From *New York Times* bestselling author Nora Roberts comes a hardcover edition of **PUBLIC SECRETS**, a tale of a pop-music superstar's daughter who grows to womanhood amid secrets too painful to remember, too dangerous to forget. From Teresa Medeiros comes **TOUCH OF ENCHANTMENT**, the sequel to her national bestseller, BREATH OF MAGIC. The only thing Tabitha Lenox hates more than being a witch is being a rich witch. But when she finds a mysterious family heirloom, she is whisked back to an era of dragons, knights, magic—and love. Newcomer Annette Reynolds delivers **REMEMBER THE TIME**, a spellbinding romance full of emotion and passion, in the tradition of Fern Michaels. When Kate Armstrong's husband dies in a tragic accident, little does she know she will learn more about him in death than she ever did while he was alive. Can Kate overcome her grief to rediscover her true self and find the love and fulfillment she deserves?

For current information on Bantam's women's fiction, visit our new web site, ISN'T IT ROMANTIC, at the following address:

http://www.bdd.com/romance

AFFAIR

by
New York Times bestselling author

Amanda Quick

available in hardcover

*Charlotte Arkendale thinks she knows all there is
to know about men. But nothing in her
experience has prepared her for Baxter St. Ives. A
dedicated man of science, St. Ives finds himself
reluctantly embroiled in a murder investigation—
and at the mercy of a fierce and highly illogical
passion for Charlotte. Caught up in their web of
passion, the lovers are unaware that a killer stalks
them, plotting to separate them . . . or to see
them joined together forever—in death.*

"You leave me no option but to be blunt, Mr. St. Ives.
Unfortunately, the truth of the matter is that you are not
quite what I had in mind in the way of a man-of-affairs."
Charlotte Arkendale clasped her hands together on top
of the wide mahogany desk and regarded Baxter with a
critical eye. "I am sorry for the waste of your time."

The interview was not going well. Baxter adjusted the
gold-framed eyeglasses on the bridge of his nose and
silently vowed that he would not give in to the impulse
to grind his back teeth.

"Forgive me, Miss Arkendale, but I was under the impression that you wished to employ a person who appeared completely innocuous and uninteresting."

"Quite true."

"I believe your exact description of the ideal candidate
for the position was, and I quote, *a person who is as bland
as a potato pudding.*"

Charlotte blinked wide, disconcertingly intelligent, green eyes. "You do not comprehend me properly, sir."

"I rarely make mistakes, Miss Arkendale. I am nothing if not precise, methodical, and deliberate in my ways. Mistakes are made by those who are impulsive or inclined toward excessive passions. I assure you, I am not of that temperament."

"I could not agree with you more on the risks of a passionate nature," she said quickly. "Indeed, that is one of the problems—"

"Allow me to read to you precisely what you wrote in your letter to your recently retired man-of-affairs."

"There is no need. I am perfectly aware of what I wrote to Mr. Marcle."

Baxter ignored her. He reached into the inside pocket of his slightly rumpled coat and removed the letter he had stored there. He had read the damn thing so many times that he almost had it memorized, but he made a show of glancing down at the flamboyant handwriting.

"'As you know, Mr. Marcle, I require a man-of-affairs to take your place. He must be a person who presents an ordinary, unassuming appearance. I want a man who can go about his business unnoticed; a gentleman with whom I can meet frequently without attracting undue attention or comment.

"'In addition to the customary duties of a man-of-affairs, duties which you have fulfilled so very admirably during the past five years, sir, I must ask that the gentleman whom you recommend possess certain other skills.

"'I shall not trouble you with the details of the situation in which I find myself. Suffice it to say that due to recent events I am in need of a stout, keenly alert individual who can be depended upon to protect my person. In short, I wish to employ a bodyguard as well as a man-of-affairs.

"'Expense, as always, must be a consideration. Therefore, rather than undertake the cost of engaging two men to fill two posts, I have concluded that it will prove more economical to employ one man who can carry out the responsibilities of both positions—'"

"Yes, yes, I recall my own words quite clearly," Charlotte interrupted testily. "But that is not the point." Baxter doggedly continued:

"'I therefore request that you send me a respectable gentleman who meets the above requirements and who presents an appearance that is as bland as a potato pudding.'"

"I fail to see why you must repeat aloud everything on the page, Mr. St. Ives." Baxter pressed on:

"'He must be endowed with a high degree of intelligence as I shall require him to make the usual delicate inquiries for me. But in his capacity as a bodyguard, he must also be skilled in the use of a pistol in case events take a nasty turn. Above all, Mr. Marcle, as you well know, he must be discreet.'"

"Enough, Mr. St. Ives." Charlotte picked up a small volume bound in red leather and slapped it smartly against the desktop to get his attention.

Baxter glanced up from the letter. "I believe I meet most of your requirements, Miss Arkendale."

"I am certain that you do meet a few of them." She favored him with a frosty smile. "Mr. Marcle would never have recommended you to me if that were not the case. Unfortunately there is one very important qualification which you lack."

Baxter deliberately refolded the letter and slipped it back inside his coat. "You insisted upon a man who would draw little attention. A staid, unremarkable man-of-affairs."

"Yes, but—"

"Allow me to tell you that I am often described in those very terms. Bland as a potato pudding in every way."

Charlotte scowled. "Do not feed me that banbury tale. You most certainly are not a potato pudding. Just the opposite, in fact."

He stared at her. "I beg your pardon?"

She groaned. "You must know very well, sir, that your spectacles are a poor disguise."

"Disguise?" He wondered if he had got the wrong address and the wrong Charlotte Arkendale. Perhaps he had got the wrong town. "What in the name of the devil do you believe me to be concealing?"

"Surely you are not suffering from the illusion that those spectacles mask your true nature."

"My true nature?" Baxter lost his grip on his patience. "Bloody hell, just what am I, if not innocuous and unprepossessing?"

She spread her hands wide. "You have the look of a man of strong passions who has mastered his temperament with even stronger powers of self-mastery."

"I beg your pardon?"

Her eyes narrowed with grim determination. "Such a man cannot hope to go about unnoticed. You are bound to attract attention when you conduct business on my behalf. I cannot have that in my man-of-affairs. I require someone who can disappear into a crowd. Someone whose face no one recalls very clearly. Don't you understand, sir? You give the appearance of being rather, well, to be quite blunt, *dangerous.*"

The nationally bestselling author of *Prince of Shadows* and *Star-Crossed* weaves a thrilling new tale of time travel, intrigue, and romantic adventure.

TWICE A HERO
by Susan Krinard

MacKenzie "Mac" Sinclair is cursed. So is the whole Sinclair family. Ever since her great-great-grandfather Peregrine returned from an expedition to the Mayan ruins with half of a mysterious pendant—and without his partner, Liam O'Shea—they've been haunted by misfortune. That's why Mac's beloved grandfather wants her to undertake a solo expedition . . . to return the pendant to the ruins of Tikal and find a way to atone for whatever part Peregrine played in Liam's disappearance. But when Mac braves the steamy, primitive jungle, something extraordinary happens: she blunders into the arms of an eerily familiar explorer. Now she's in for more adventure than she bargained for. Because she's found Liam O'Shea . . . alive, well, and seductively real. In the year 1884.

The woman was obviously an actress of considerable talent. Or she was quite mad.

"1884?" she repeated, her low voice hoarse. "Did you say—*1*884? But that's not possible."

Liam regarded her stunned expression with suspicious bemusement. Simple insanity did fit hand in glove with the rest of her: thin, wiry, distinctly peculiar with her cap of short hair and bold dark eyes, sharp-tongued, dressed top to toe in men's clothing of an odd cut, and carrying a newfangled electric lantern the likes of which he had never seen in all his travels. And alone here in the jungle, first claiming she'd been with a full party of explorers and then insisting that no man had brought her.

And then there were her odd manner of speech, her absurd assertions of hotels in the jungle and omnibuses from Flores, her reaction to Tikal—as if she'd expected to see something entirely different, though she claimed to know the ruins.

Yes, one could almost believe she was in a state of mental disturbance—if not for the photograph she had so carelessly allowed him to see. The one taken here in these very ruins four years ago.

"What did you expect, Miss MacKenzie?" he asked. "Maybe you've been in the jungle too long after all."

Her dark brows drew down, and her gaze grew unfocused. "Okay, Mac," she muttered. "Time to wake up. This isn't happening."

Was this act a way of protecting herself, avoiding his questions because she'd revealed too much? Liam couldn't forget the shock he'd felt when he'd seen her with the photograph. Until that moment she'd been only an unforeseen burden to dispose of in the nearest safe place, some eccentric suffragist amateur explorer who'd been lost or deliberately abandoned, left for him to save.

After what had happened yesterday, he'd never considered doing otherwise.

The sharp sting of recent memory made the bitterness rise in his throat: Perry's revelation, the knowledge that Liam's trust in his partner had been entirely misplaced, the fight, drinking to drown the rage and loss, waking up this morning to find the bearers, mules, and nearly all the supplies, gone. With Perry.

Abandoned. Betrayed by the one man he'd thought he could trust. The man who stood beside him in that damned photograph.

He'd thought the girl in far more desperate straits than himself. She was of the weaker sex, in spite of her ridiculous beliefs to the contrary. But now—now he felt a grinding suspicion in his gut, wild thoughts fully as mad as the woman's incoherent ramblings and disjointed explanations.

Liam scowled at Miss MacKenzie's inward stare. She wasn't the only one with wits gone begging. A woman? Even Perry wouldn't sink so far. And there hadn't been time. But after yesterday nothing seemed beyond possibility.

And their meeting had seemed more than merely coincidence.

He studied her, chin on fist, allowing himself full rein to his imagination. Perry would never assume that his erstwhile partner would be distracted by a woman like this. She was hardly beautiful. Her hair was ridiculously short, her brows too heavy, her stubborn jaw too strong, her figure too narrow. Though she'd proven she was, in fact, female enough when the rain had soaked through her shirt.

He found himself gazing at her chest. More there than he'd first noticed; come to think of it, she couldn't pass for a boy, not unless that loose shirt were completely dry. . . .

You've been without a woman too long, O'Shea. He snorted. *No.* At best Perry would expect him to be delayed further, getting the girl back to civilization. That would neatly fit in with his intentions.

Liam's fist slammed into the wet stone of the temple. Perry knew too damned much about him. He knew Liam wouldn't leave any woman alone in the jungle, no matter what his circumstances—without supplies or bearers or even a single scrawny mule. . . .

Because you trusted him. The rage bubbled up again, and with very little effort he could imagine his fist connecting with Perry's superior, aristocratic face.

By the saints, it wasn't over yet. When Liam got back to San Francisco—

"That's it."

He snapped out of his grim reverie. Miss MacKenzie—"Mac," the name she had called herself and which suited her so well—had apparently recovered her senses. Or ended her game. She was on her feet, looking out over the jungle with set jaw and a lunatic's obsession.

"I'm going back," she announced.

Liam rose casually. The top of her cropped head came almost to his chin; tall for a woman. He hadn't realized that before.

"Back where—'Mac'?" he drawled.

Her stare was no longer unfocused. She looked at him as if she'd like to pitch him over the side of the pyramid. "Only my friends call me Mac," she said, "and you're sure as hell not my friend. You're a figment of my over-heated imagination."

He gave a startled bark of laughter. Whoever and whatever she was, she had the ridiculous ability to make him hover between laughter and outrage. No woman had ever managed that before. She was too damned good at keeping him off balance. Was that her purpose—and Perry's?

To hell with that. If there was anything to his suspicions, he'd learn soon enough.

"So," he said, "you don't think I'm real?" He took one long step, closing the gap between them, and felt her shudder as his chest brushed hers. He could feel the little tips of her breasts, hardening through the shirt. He felt an unexpected hardening in his own body. "What proof do you need, eh?"

She tried to step back, but the temple wall was behind her. "You . . . uh . . ." She thrust out her jaw and glared. "Let me by. I'm going back to the ruins."

"If I'm not real, Mac, you should have no difficulty walking through me."

Suddenly she chuckled. The sound had a hysterical edge. "Great idea," she said. With the full force of her slender weight she pushed against him. The assault drove him back a pace. She stepped to the side, strode to the rim of the temple platform, and slid her foot over the edge.

He caught her arm just as an ancient stone step gave way under her foot. "Are you so eager to break your neck?" he snapped. "Or are you more afraid of something else?"

Her eyes were wide and dark and surprisingly large, rimmed with thick lashes he hadn't noticed before. There was a slight trembling to the lids and at the corners of her lips, as if she'd realized how easy it would have been to tumble down that steep incline in her reckless attempt to escape.

Escape *him*. Was that what she was trying to do?

From the delightful, passionate voice of

Adrienne deWolfe

author of *Texas Outlaw* and *Texas Lover*
comes

TEXAS WILDCAT

*Bailey McShane has had a crush on Zack Rawlins
since she was thirteen and he was courting her
cousin. Now, nearly ten years later, she and Zack
hardly seem able to exchange a civil word with
each other. Bailey knows that is partly due to a
severe drought in Texas, which has been setting
sheepherders—like herself—against cattle
ranchers—like Zack. But Bailey is sure she and
Zack can at least be friends; so when he comes to
her ranch one day with a peace offering, she
gladly invites him to stay for dinner—a dinner
that ends with them both drinking too much
moonshine as a storm gathers overhead. . . .*

"Rain," Bailey whispered.

She jumped to her feet and ran a bit unsteadily to the
window, planting her hands on the sill and sticking her
head and shoulders outside. When she turned her face
to the skies, wind kicked up her sheaf of hair, and thunder crashed like two colliding locomotives, shaking the
wooden frame around her. She giggled like a child.

"Rain!" she shouted, turning to face Zack, her cheeks
streaked by the droplets that were sliding into her collar.
"Let's go watch!"

Before he could draw breath enough to answer, she
grabbed the room's lone lamp and raced into the pitch
blackness of the hallway.

Thrown into darkness, Zack muttered an oath, not waiting for his eyes to grow accustomed before he pushed back his chair. The moonshine hit him full force then, and his knees wobbled. The very idea that some slip of a sheepherder was holding her liquor better than he was was enough to make the blood rush to his head. He grabbed his hat and fanned his face.

"C'mon, Zack!"

Her voice floated in to him above the banging of the front door, and he grinned. He couldn't help it. Rain, by God. There was actually rain!

Draping his Stetson haphazardly over his brow, he hurried across the unfamiliar floor, banging his shin on the doorstop and stubbing his toe on a sitting-room chair. He hardly noticed, though. He was too eager to follow that beckoning light to the circle of brightness it cast on the parched and withered yard. Bailey had balanced the lamp on the porch railing, and when he pushed open the bottom half of the door, he spied her dancing in its yellow blaze. Laughing, she spun like a top, her arms outstretched, her face turned to the heavens. He stumbled to a halt, simply staring.

Her exuberance had loosed her hair from its leather thong, and it whipped around her like slick amber tongues, twining around her upper arms, slapping her buttocks, caressing her thighs. The rain had plastered her jeans to her skin, and the white cotton of her shirt was growing nigh transparent. He swallowed hard, unable to do the gentlemanly thing, unable to tear his gaze away from that sheer clinging fabric and the feminine peaks and valleys it outlined so faithfully.

She crooked her forefinger at him in a beckoning gesture. "C'mere, cowboy," she said huskily.

"What for?" he drawled, stepping off the porch.

"So I can do . . . *this*!"

Before he could guess her intention, she snatched the Stetson from his head and dashed away, whooping like an Indian in a rain dance.

"Hey!" He couldn't stop himself from laughing. "Give me back my hat, woman!"

"Not unless you catch me first!"

"I'll catch you, all right," he growled, and charged after her.

Her heels clattered on the planks of the bridge. In a flash of lightning, he saw her balanced precariously on the bridge's railless edge. He was just about to rush to her when he heard her gasp. Suddenly she wobbled. Her arms and legs flailed. In the next instant she was toppling, shrieking at the top of her lungs.

"Bailey!"

Without thought for his boots or spurs, Zack ran for the stream bank. Slipping and sliding, he scrambled through the rain-slickened reeds and plunged into the water. All he could think in that terrible, mind-numbing moment was that he'd lost her. He'd lost his precious Bailey.

Then he heard a splash.

It was followed by a giggle.

A shadow rose before him, slipping water in cascades, dumping another hatful over itself when it crammed the Stetson onto its head.

"That was fun!" the shadow shouted cheerfully.

Well, that was it. The final straw. Zack grabbed her arm, which threw them both off balance, and they landed side by side in about two feet of water. With a feral sound that was half frustration and half mirth, he fastened his lips over hers, drawing her tongue deep into his mouth. With a hunger he hadn't realized he possessed, he tasted and feasted, plundering the hot, wet mystery behind her breaths. His craving grew more insistent, more demanding with each intoxicating moment.

"Bailey," he groaned, struggling to remember his code of honor, struggling to beat back the desire that crackled along his electrified nerves. "We have to . . . You need to . . . It's time you dried off."

He boosted her to her feet, then hoisted her into his arms.

"Where are you taking me?" she asked, sounding childlike and uncertain as he waded toward the reeds.

"Inside, out of the rain."

"What for?"

"So you can change your wet clothes."

She seemed to think about that for a moment, worrying her bottom lip. Then she loosed a dreamy sigh and dropped her head against his shoulder. "Good. I always wanted you to be the one, Zack. . . ."

From the *New York Times* bestselling
author of **Montana Sky**

NORA ROBERTS

creates a classic suspense tale of a father's
betrayal and a daughter's quest for

SWEET REVENGE

Now available in paperback

The child of a fabled Hollywood star and a
charming, titled playboy, Princess Adrianne
lives a life most people would envy. But her
pampered-rich-girl pose is a ruse . . . a
carefully calculated effort to hide a dangerous
truth. For ten years, Adrianne has lived for
revenge. As a child, she could only watch the
cruelty hidden behind the facade of her parents' fairy-tale marriage. Now, though nothing will bring her mother back, Adrianne is
ready to make her father pay. As the infa-
mous jewel thief, The Shadow, Adrianne is
poised to steal the Sun and Moon—a neck-
lace beyond price—and to taste the sweetness
of her long-sought revenge . . . until she
meets a man who seems to divine her every
secret—and has his own private reasons for
getting close to Princess Adrianne.

On sale in June

TOUCH OF ENCHANTMENT
by Teresa Medeiros

REMEMBER THE TIME
by Annette Reynolds

PUBLIC SECRETS
by Nora Roberts